CW00865207

SUMMER IN SAN SEBASTIAN

Joy Skye

CONTENTS

CHAPTER ONE

From: Adamflynn@sublimeretreats.com

To: PedroZubiri@donostiaestates.es

Subject: San Sebastian Acquisition Schedule

Dear Pedro,

Further to our conversation yesterday, I can confirm that Mr Williams and I will travel to Spain in the second week of April in order to select the property we require for Sublime Retreats. After the success of Florence's launch, we are keen to hit the ground running as soon as we find the perfect apartment and have already started marketing the destination.

We will only be there for three days, so we want to visit as many places as possible. Please find the requirements list attached, and we will be making a decision before we leave. Sublime Retreats aim to start booking guests in the first week of next month, so your assistance in finding a concierge and local tours etc. is greatly appreciated.

Any questions, please just ask, and I will send you our flight details shortly.

Best regards,

Adam

Adam Flynn

Acquisitions Manager

Sublime Retreats

Abigail leaned back in the hard blue and yellow seat, closing her eyes to surrounding chaos, and tried not to think of the life she was leaving behind. Six months ago, she had a job she loved, a fiancé she thought she loved, and a rather nice flat in Clapham Junction. Now she was on a plane, going to see Mad Aunt May in Spain because it felt like the only option left available to her. She opened her eyes briefly to watch the safety video, as the plane taxied towards take-off, then firmly closed them again, to make it all go away.

She only opened them when the flight attendant asked if she wanted a drink. The stale smell of scalded coffee that permeated the cabin made her decision easy. 'A large gin and tonic please,' she said emphatically, conscious that it was 11 am but not giving a damn. Ignoring his expression of disapproval, she took the plastic cup from him with her biggest smile, looked at his nametag and said acerbically, 'thank you so much, Craig. It's a pleasure to be *served* by you today.'

Taking a long sip from the cup, Abigail let out a sigh of relief. A quick pit stop in Madrid, then another short hop, and she'd be in San Sebastian. She had always wanted to go. Her aunt's descriptions of the place sounded amazing, but she had never quite got around to it, a fact that she felt guilty about. Especially as May was welcoming her now, without hesitation and with open arms, despite her vagabond status.

'Just hop on a plane, darling,' had been her aunt's immediate response to her call. 'Get yourself over here for some sun and Sangria. We can sort out everything else later.' May continued, even though Abigail hesitated, unsure if this was the right thing to do. 'Bite the biscuit sweetie, no point crying over spilt gin!'

Laughing at May's constant inability to get even the simplest idiom right, she had agreed. Maybe a few weeks in another country with a better climate was just what she needed. A couple of clicks on the phone later and she'd spent the last of her savings on the flights that would get her to the sanctuary of Mad Aunt May and San Sebastian.

She dozed, the gin kicking in, but the rather large man with the sad comb-over in the seat next to her kept oozing over the armrest and invading her minimal space. The second flight found her thankfully with an empty seat next to her so she could relax a little more and she perked up, feeling her spirits lift as she watched the landscape undulate and transform beneath them.

As the plane started its descent, banking over the cerulean blue sea, and sweeping effortlessly around, she glimpsed a swathe of golden sand. A jumble of white buildings with terracotta roofs backed it, crammed onto the spit of land, and then the runway appeared as if by magic, and they were touching down.

After the interminable wait for passport control - Brexit had a lot to answer for - she joined the crowds hustling to get to baggage claim and stood by idly watching the conveyor belt as brightly coloured suitcases started their lap, waiting to be leapt upon by frantic tourists who seemed to think that they would disappear forever if not immediately snapped up.

Thankfully, she soon saw the enormous backpack that Emma had lent her, a leftover from her friend's younger, more carefree days, and elbowed through the mob to grab it. Heaving the bag containing most of her worldly possessions onto her back, she wound her way through the airport, following the signs for the exit.

The brilliant sunshine that greeted her had her rummaging through her handbag for her sunglasses. Unfortunately, that was the only thing that greeted her; there was no sign of May anywhere. Abigail wandered back inside and found a shop to buy a bottle of water. She was travel parched and drained it in three big gulps. Refreshed, she popped the empty bottle in a nearby bin as she walked back outside, but there was still no sign of her aunt. Already too warm and sweating slightly, she plonked her bag on a bench in the shade of the airport canopy, took off her padded jacket, and dug her phone out, fanning her face as she did so.

'Aunt May, it's Abi,' she said when the call was answered.

'Oh Abi, lovely to hear from you. I am so looking forward to seeing you!' Aunt May exclaimed.

'Me too. That's why I'm calling. I'm here, standing outside the airport.'

'Is that today, darling? Oh my, I am so forgetful. Listen, just give me fifteen minutes or so and I'll be there to get you. We can go for some lunch. How's that?'

Resigning herself to the wait, Abigail settled on the bench and scrolled through her phone to see what the rest of the world was up to. A post from Jason's Instagram came into view; it was a video of him and his new girlfriend, shooting a confetti cannon. Pink scraps of fluttering paper sprayed across the park. #itsagirl

She couldn't believe her eyes; the bitter taste of bile rose in her throat. They had discussed having a baby many times, but Jason had always said they should wait. Wait until they were more financially stable, wait until they could buy a house, wait until she found another job. There had always been an excuse. She had an overwhelming sense of betrayal, far bigger than when she had found out he had been cheating on her, and huge, ugly, all-consuming sobs wracked her. It was only when she felt arms around her that she realised her aunt had arrived.

'There, there,' May murmured soothingly, holding her close and smoothing her hair until the deluge faded. Looking up at her aunt through blurry eyes, Abi managed a wan smile. Aunt May looked exactly as she remembered her. The grey hair, streaked with silver now, was still wild, curly and uncontrollable, despite being firmly pressed down by a large, bright yellow floppy hat. Her trademark, faded kaftan splattered with splashes of paint, her neck was adorned with rows of multicoloured beads and her feet were ensconced in the ever-ugly clogs she insisted on wearing.

Her steely blue eyes had a twinkle in them as she studied her niece's pale face for a beat.
'You will get through this, Abi. However bad things seem right now, this is just a tiny blip in what will be a lifetime of happiness.'

Nodding gratefully, Abi wiped her tears with the back of her hands, trying to regain control. 'Thanks, Aunt May,' she sniffed. 'Sorry, I just had a bit of a moment there.'

'Well, it's always darkest before the prawn. Let's go somewhere nice for lunch and get some alcohol inside you,' she said firmly, taking her by the hand and pulling her to her feet. Feeling a little better, she laughed as she hoisted on the heavy blue rucksack and followed Aunt May to her ancient campervan.

'I can't believe this old thing is still going,' said Abi as she slid open the back to put her bag in. The washed-out green paint of the old VW showed the various artworks that had been added to it over the years and Abi could see there had been some additions since she last saw it. Brightly coloured flowers and butterflies in primrose yellow and baby doll pink now cavorted around the slogan *make love, not war*, a reminder of another era and her aunt's more youthful adventures.

'Us old gals will keep going together, Bessie and me, 'till the end, darling,' she said defiantly as she turned the key. The engine sputtered to life with a belch of smoke that had bystanders choking for air as they chugged away.

As they left the airport and drove towards the city, Abi was grateful that her aunt wasn't insisting on talking. Seemingly happy, she was humming away to herself as she careered around the bends. Clutching the sides of the seat for dear life, Abi looked out the window, trying to take in the landscape as a distraction from the impending, seemingly inevitable collision. The scenery became greener as they left the airport's industrial surroundings and rolling hills arose, checkered with houses that had a decidedly French air which Abi realised was unsurprising, being so close to the border.

The city skyline had appeared on the horizon, nestling at the base of the mountains that framed it, when she spotted a group of protesters by an expanse of land, wielding signs, with writing daubed on in various coloured paints. She could hear their muted chanting as they marched around and around in angry circles.

'What's going on there?' she glanced at Aunt May to see if she was aware of them.

'Oh, those horrible developers are trying to buy that land and build on the nature reserve!' replied May angrily. 'We've been fighting it for months, that's where I was when you called.'

'A nature reserve? How on earth can they get permission to build there?'

'It's big business and more than a little "graisser la patte",' said May with a faux French accent as they sped wide around another bend, causing an approaching car to swerve and toot in alarm.

'Graisser whaty?' asked Abi, amazed as ever at her aunt's multilingual abilities.

'Greasing the qualms,' May fumed with a scowl, causing Abi to laugh for the first time in days.

'What? What are you laughing at? This is serious,' May said a little huffily.

'It's supposed to be... Oh, never mind. Your version is pretty accurate,' Abi said, smiling at her dippy aunt. 'Anyway, where are we going for lunch? I'm famished,' she said, realising it was true as she mentioned it. She couldn't remember the last time she'd eaten anything substantial. It was probably before she found out about Jason and *her.*

'You've never been to Spain before, have you, Abi?' said May, going on before her niece could answer. 'I am going to take you to the best pintxo place in town so you can experience the real deal!'

With a look at May's gleeful face, Abi refrained from investigating that statement any further. She had no idea what pintxos were, but was looking forward to finding out and just settled back to enjoy the ride. She had come here to escape, and she was determined to enjoy every single minute of it.

They cruised through the busy roads of the centre, narrowly missing buses and pedestrians alike, before reaching the seafront, and May turned right along the promenade. It was a relief when they screeched into a parking area and the van drew up with a judder as May yanked up the hand brake.

'Here we are,' she announced gaily, unstrapping herself and hauling her large handbag out from the rear. Gratefully stretching her legs as she got out, Abi took in a deep breath of the salty air and turned her face to the sun. Even though it was only April, the warmth was there. So unlike the cold, damp of England that she had left behind in such haste this morning, she thought, smiling to herself.

'Come on, you,' called May, 'it's just a short walk

from here.'

As they strolled companionably along the seafront, Abi could hear tinkling music playing in the distance. When they got closer to the sound, she looked on in delight at the Victorian-looking carousel spinning its relentless rounds. The few children that were riding it looked rapt, their little faces glowing in the flashing lights, while proud parents looked on.

'That's beautiful,' she said, enchanted, glancing at May. 'How old is it?'

Aunt May laughed merrily, obviously just as taken with it, even though she had no doubt seen it countless times before.

'It is actually a replica of the original. Back in its heyday, San Sebastian was a veritable city of entertainment and the local council was trying to reproduce that golden era when they built this.'

As she glanced around at the fairly quiet streets and the empty beach, Abi could see that they hadn't quite succeeded. Seeing her expression, May asserted, 'don't let the appearance of peace fool you. In a few weeks, the season will kick off and you won't recognise the place!'

They continued walking and May led them confidently through the narrow, cobbled backstreets, which were growing busier the deeper they went into the old city, until they came to the restaurant she was aiming for. Baztan Pintxos & Bar was a small, traditional-looking place with a jam-packed bar area, but that didn't put May off.

'In here,' she called, grabbing Abi by the hand and pulling her through the throng to the counter. Under the glare of the overhead lights, she could see an incredible array of dishes with enticing looking delicacies stretching out and disappearing around the corner. The air was redolent with delicious smells of grilled meats and garlic and something else she didn't recognise.

'*Kaixo*, May!' called a tall, extremely handsome barman, bustling up. 'What can I get you today?'

'Hi, Miquel,' she replied easily. 'This is my niece Abigail, she's going to be staying here for a while, so I thought I'd introduce her to the best-looking barman in Donata,' she added coquettishly, causing Abi to blush on her behalf. But he just laughed good-naturedly, unperturbed by May's flirtations, as he dried his hands on a towel and put it to one side.

'Lovely to meet you, Abigail,' he said, his eyes roaming her body and taking in her curves in a flash. 'I think your aunt means she is going to introduce you to the best food in town.'

'Yes, yes, that too,' said Aunt May with a giggle as Abi crossed her arms self-consciously over her chest.

'How about you give us a selection of today's specials? But make sure you include the veal cheek and the squid. You know how much I adore them! And pour us a couple of beers to wash it down with.'

A short while later, plates arrived on the counter in front of them, containing morsels of food spiked with cocktail sticks and a handful of napkins on the side. Abi's stomach grumbled at the sight and she dived in, not caring what she was eating, despite the previous mention of veal cheeks.
Washing down the first mouthfuls with a couple of gulps of the cold beer, she relaxed for the first time that day and took in her surroundings with interest. The place was bustling with a mixed crowd, the air vibrant with conversation.

'This is a great place for people watching,' she said to her aunt, who was busy cramming mouthfuls of food down with gusto. Aunt May nodded while she tried to swallow. 'It sure is,' she mumbled indistinctly, wiping her mouth before taking a breath. 'Most of the places around here are great for watching the world go by. I much prefer them to the overpriced bars on the seafront.'

There was a pause while she took another bite before asking gently, 'so are you going to tell me exactly what happened?'

Abi stopped, food halfway to her mouth, and looked at May. She deserved to know what had brought her niece scurrying to Spain in such a hurry, but Abi wasn't ready to talk about it yet.

'Do you mind if I don't?' she appealed hopefully with a sad smile.

'Of course, darling, I am not going to force you to talk about painful things, although it's always better out than in. How about we talk about what you are going to do while you are here?'

'I hadn't really thought about it,' she answered honestly. 'I just needed to get away, and this seemed like the best place I could go.'

'Well, I am thrilled to see you for whatever reason,' her aunt replied with her usual sunny smile. 'But I think we need to find you something to do. There's only so much sightseeing one can do, as lovely as it is here. Maybe we can find something at the estate agents where I work for you. It's getting busier now. I'll ask Pedro if there's something you can help out with.'

'I can't lie. I spent pretty much the last of my money on the plane ticket to get here, so if I could earn a little something that would be marvellous,' said Abi, her spirits lifting at the idea. Having been out of work for six months after the party planning company she worked for let her go, she was at her wits' end financially.

'You don't have to worry about money for now,' said May, squeezing her arm. 'I'm fairly comfortable. My last exhibition went well, and I sold most of the paintings. As it happens, I have another one coming up at the beginning of next month. So, you could help me with organising that if you like? I'm not very good with the finer details, you know, like sending invites, booking caterers, all the boring stuff.'

'I'd be thrilled to,' replied Abi, leaning forward, her eyes lighting up. 'After all, organising things for other people is basically what I have done for the last decade of my life. It will be fantastic to do it for someone I love for a change!'

Happy to see some life in her niece, May picked up her glass and raised it in a toast. 'Here's to your summer in San Sebastian, whatever it may bring!'

CHAPTER TWO

Gabe Xavier stood in his office looking at the misty Manhattan skyline as dusk blanketed the buildings and rubbed his temples. It had been a long day, and he was glad it was coming to an end. He heard the door open as his assistant, Marianna, came in with another sheaf of papers for him to read and sign.

'Is there anything else you need, sir?' she asked hopefully as she placed them on his desk, her eyes greedily running down the length of his rangy frame before settling back on his handsome face.

'No, I'm fine. Get yourself home,' he retorted, not even glancing at her. Once he heard the door softly close, he strode over to the built-in bar and poured himself a neat bourbon before sitting in the leather chair behind his desk and loosening his tie with a sigh. He was exhausted. The deal he had closed today was the culmination of three months of hard slog, but he had finally got the answer he was looking for. He touched a button on the controller on his desk and the office lights dimmed, highlighting the skyline view from the windows.

Idly flicking through his emails, he saw one from Sublime Retreats, the holiday club he had a gold membership with. He mostly used them to wine and dine clients, weekends up in Denver skiing, snorkelling in Cabo. The luxury services and properties offered by the club always impressed everyone; it was a useful tool to close a deal. Showing people what money could buy you was always an excellent incentive to get them to accept whatever he was offering.

He opened the email with a swift click and was almost blinded by the pictures of bright sunny beaches, bustling bars with suave looking patrons and an ancient carousel doing its rounds before an endlessly blue sea. San Sebastian, the headline proudly announced, is the newest addition to our much sought-after City Breaks program. *Book your slot now to avoid disappointment!*

Gabe stared at the images for a moment, running a hand through his short blonde hair. He was drawn to something there but couldn't figure it out. Marketing tactics seldom took him in, he was the king of sales, after all. He knew a hook when he saw it, but the colourful pictures scrolling across his screen called to him.

His phone sounded, startling him out of his reverie, and he glanced at the caller ID before answering with another sigh.

'Hi Natasha, I was just thinking about you,' he lied smoothly, taking a sip of his drink.

'Hi Gabe,' she purred in her Southern drawl that had seemed so charming when he met her a few months ago. 'I haven't seen you for days,' she pouted down the line.

Inwardly wincing, he purposely kept his voice even. 'You know how busy I've been, babe. I told you how important this last piece of land was.'

'More important than me?' she simpered, causing his blood to run cold.

Impulsively he replied, 'look, I'm still going to be busy for the next few weeks but how about a trip to Spain in May?'

There was a pause. He could almost hear her brain ticking. Natasha didn't cope well with sudden ideas. 'Spain?' she asked faintly, as if unsure where it was.

'Yes, Spain. That's what I said.'

'But I'm lonely now. I miss you. My body misses you.' Which conjured up an image of her sleek form that he couldn't ignore. Glancing at the time, he considered his options and the implications. 'Give me half an hour,' he declared after a momentary pause and cut the call.

As the car took him to Natasha's apartment, he mused about her. He should cut her loose. She obviously believed there was more to this relationship than he was prepared to give, would ever be prepared to give. But tonight, he would celebrate his current success and worry about what came next with her tomorrow.

'Wait for me, I won't be long,' he told the driver when they pulled up outside the shabby apartment block where she lived and he strode into the building.

The next morning, when he woke up in his apartment to the smell of freshly brewed coffee, he stretched luxuriantly in the oversized bed he'd had made to accommodate his tall frame. He rose and went to the bathroom, stepping into the shower, and as he turned the jets on full blast, the images from yesterday's email started whirling around his brain again. There was something about San Sebastian that was still calling to him, and he was keen to discover exactly what it was. Roughly towelling himself dry, he wrapped the towel loosely around his waist and sauntered into the kitchen where his maid, Maria, was bustling around, preparing breakfast at the stove.

'Good morning, Maria,' he called, causing her to spin around in surprise, then drop her spatula at the sight of his naked torso and well-formed abs. Grinning to himself, he ignored the blush that swept up her face and poured a large mug of coffee, the first of many that would see him through the day. Wandering into the lounge, he fired up his laptop and looked again at San Sebastian.

Several hours later, after breakfast, he called Adam Flynn, the acquisitions manager at Sublime Retreats, with whom he'd had dealings with in the past. Locating several prime real estate properties for Sublime Retreats had been lucrative for both sides, and they had developed an uneasy friendship as a result.

'Morning, Adam,' he said with no preamble. 'Put me down for the San Sebastian slot. I want to be there as soon as the program opens next month.'

'Hi, Gabe,' Adam replied blearily, taken aback at the demand at this time of the morning. 'It's not like you to want to go abroad.'

'Well, now I do. Make it happen,' he said and closed the call, knowing full well that his wishes would be catered for. Humming to himself, he dressed in his favourite dark blue Armani and, checking his reflection with a grin, he tousled his hair for a moment before grabbing his bag and taking the lift down to the busy street.

Gabe slipped into the backseat of the waiting car and directed his driver to take him to the office, his mind running over the exciting idea that had sprouted this morning. The anticipation of doing something new was energising, and he couldn't wait to put his plan into action.

'Hold all my calls, Marianna,' he called as he went

through the reception, leaving her to trot after him with the list of messages she had faithfully typed out. He took them from her with a nod and closed his office door firmly and continued with his research. A short while later, his phone rang.

'I thought I said to hold all calls?' he answered, annoyed at the interruption.

'I know, Mr Xavier, but it's Father Thomas,' his assistant murmured.

'Put him through.'

'Good morning, my boy. How are you on this fine day?' the jovial priest enquired when Gabe greeted him.

'Everything is going great, Father T,' replied Gabe with a broad smile lighting up his face. 'How is the fundraising going?'

The priest replied with a chuckle. 'You always got straight to the crux of the matter, Gabe, even as a boy.'

'Well, life's too short for anything else, in my opinion. How much are you missing to replace the roof?'

'$100,000,' Father Thomas replied bluntly. 'We have done our best, but there's only so many bake sales you can hold.'

'Consider it done,' said Gabe amiably. 'And are you free for dinner tonight? I have an idea I would like to float past you.'

'I'm honoured, and of course, I always have time for

you, my son.'

'Excellent, 8 pm at our usual?'

'Can you make it a little earlier? These old bones like to be in bed by nine!'

Laughing, Gabe responded, 'no problem, I'll see you there at six.' Putting his phone down with a smile, he noticed a message from Natasha, causing his smile to drop as he remembered his promise last night to take her to Spain. *That I will deal with later*, he thought to himself, making a mental note to get Marianna to send the usual bouquet with the well-used note of regret that had stood him in good stead for so long.

That evening he arrived at La Famiglia, their favourite Italian restaurant, a few minutes early, to be greeted with a warm welcome from Sergio the owner, and to find Father Thomas already seated in a booth, nursing a glass of red wine. The old priest beamed when he saw Gabe, and placing his hands on the table, pushed himself upright. Gabe couldn't help but notice how wizened the man looked. He seemed to have shrunk in the few months since he'd last seen him.
The sparse silver hair and beard that framed his round face were noticeably wispier, and the crow's feet that fanned out from his eyes deeper and more pronounced. But the grey eyes behind the glasses still twinkled with merriment as he stood to greet him.

'Gabe, my boy,' he said, embracing him with affection. 'Cutting a dashing figure as ever, I see,' the old fellow laughed, pulling back and looking him up and down.

'I dress to impress, Father T,' he countered, nodding at Sergio's enquiry as to his usual drink. 'How are things at Francis Xavier? Did you get the funds I wired through?'

'Yes, we did. God bless you. Work will start on the roof in a few weeks. The children in the orphanage are very grateful to you, Gabe, as am I.'

'Don't mention it,' he replied, taking a sip from the glass of bourbon that had arrived in front of him. 'After everything you have done for me, it's the least I can do.'

Sensing Gabe's discomfort and knowing full well he would not discuss the events of his childhood, Father Thomas opted to change the subject.

'So, how are things? I mean, in your personal life; the entire world knows how successful your business is! How's... I want to say Natalie?' he suggested, his face screwed up in concentration as he tried to recall the last media post he'd seen of Gabe arriving at some fancy do, with a long-legged blonde on his arm.

Laughing, Gabe replied, 'it was Natasha, and I am afraid we have gone our separate ways.'

'Another one bites the dust? Honestly, Gabe. When

are you going to settle down, find someone to share your life with?'

'I don't need to share my life with anyone,' he replied sullenly, looking very much like the small boy Father Thomas remembered so well. Hiding his emotions behind an attitude and a snarky comment rather than risk being hurt. Again.

'Well, I pray that one day soon you will meet someone who will change your mind,' and before Gabe could object, he picked up the menu.

'I am in the mood for the cannelloni, how about you?'

Taking the cue, he picked up his menu as well, and they placed their orders and were soon chatting over delicious plates of food. Gabe had opted for the Fiorentina steak, cooked perfectly rare, and he ate steadily as the father brought him up to date on some of the children he had grown up with.
He only had a mild interest in such news, but the old man always seemed to take such enjoyment from sharing the other's successes or setbacks, so he listened attentively as he ate.

'We have our annual get-together coming up next month,' said Father Thomas as he carefully placed his cutlery on his empty plate. 'You should come along. Everyone would love to see you.'

'I will probably be away,' said Gabe, without missing a beat. 'That reminds me, I wanted to tell you about an idea I have had.'

So, he launched into a rundown of San Sebastian, of what he had discovered there, and his plans. His face was lit with excitement and his enthusiasm shone through as he told Father Thomas all about it, making him appear more boyish than ever. He always enjoyed running his ideas past the priest. The old man had no real business acumen, so there was never any judgement on that score, but he always had a unique take on the situation.

'I have to say I'm impressed,' replied Father Thomas when he'd finished. 'This sounds like a marvellous idea. Spain, huh? Maybe you can find a little time to relax while you're there? It's about time you gave yourself a break, Gabe. I do worry about your never-ending desire to take over the world.'

'My never-ending desire to take over the world has got you a new roof, Father,' Gabe snapped, looking immediately contrite. 'Sorry,' he muttered, looking down at his hands.

'I am not denying your work ethic is a good thing,' the priest replied gently. 'But Gabe, you need to enjoy the journey. Live a little, you know?'

'I enjoy my life,' Gabe responded automatically, but pulled up short at the expression of concern on the face of the one person who was the only constant in his life. So, after a moment he added, 'but I promise to take time to enjoy myself while I'm there, ok?'

He reached across and placed his hand over the

priest's that was resting on the table, the paper-thin skin reminding him yet again how old the man was. Pushing that thought away quickly, he smiled at him. 'I'll get the bill. It's nearly your bedtime,' he said with a chuckle.

Back in his apartment, as he brushed his teeth, Gabe considered what Father Thomas had said about finding someone to share his life with. The old man just did not understand that he could not open himself up to that possibility. That he was perfectly fine by himself, just as he always had been, and there was no reason to rock that particular boat, was there?

CHAPTER THREE

Aunt May's home was charming. Utterly chaotic, but charming. She owned the top two floors of a rambling old apartment block in Egia, with views across the rooftops to the sea in the distance, and had put her distinctive stamp on the place. Each room was a splash of colour, crammed with an eclectic selection of furniture, all flea market finds. The walls were peppered with a jumble of pictures, all mismatched styles and sizes.

Books lined the rest of the available space, even spilling into the cluttered kitchen that currently contained Mad Aunt May, still in her bathrobe and slippers, singing along to 'Born to be Wild' loudly and out of tune, with great enjoyment.

'Good morning,' called Abi, when there was a pause in the soundtrack.

'Good morning, sweetheart. How did you sleep?' her aunt smiled at her as she whisked a bowl of eggs in a large glass bowl held in the crook of one arm.

'Like a log,' said Abi, coming to sit on one of the zebra print stools by the counter. 'Best sleep I've had in weeks,' she added with a smile.

'Glad to hear it! We have a busy day today. I am going to take you to see the space where my next exhibition will be and then we shall go to see Pedro and find out if he can offer you some work.'

'That sounds perfect,' she responded eagerly, leaning her elbows on the counter.

After months of sloth, Abigail felt thrilled to have a plan of action. When she'd called Aunt May, she simply had not known what else she could do. But it was looking to be a good call, not the act of desperation it had felt at the time. Losing her job had been gut-wrenching, if not entirely unexpected in the pandemic's aftermath. Discovering that Jason was a two-timing tosser had been the final nail in the coffin of her life as she knew it.

Ten days ago, she had decided to snap out of her fugue caused by a lack of work and purpose. She'd got herself up, showered and dressed, cleaned the apartment and set out to go to Sainsbury's to get some shopping in so she could cook them something for dinner for the first time in ages. Cutting across the park, she had stopped dead in her tracks at the sight of a familiar silhouette on a bench.

It was Jason, and he wasn't alone. He was sitting there bold as brass, holding the hand of another woman. When he leaned in and they started snogging, Abigail didn't hang around to see what was coming next. She ran straight home to their flat, packed a bag and turned up unannounced on her friend Emma's doorstep in floods of tears.

A bottle of Merlot and a drunken phone call later revealed that Jason had been seeing this other girl for 6 months, but had felt unable to tell her as she had been so depressed.
'So, it's my bloody fault, is it?' she had screeched down the phone. Not her finest moment.

So here she was. Despite Emma's protestations that they could make do in her tiny one-bed flat, Abigail had called the only person in the world who could possibly help. Mad Aunt May.

A loud screech cut through the apartment and her thoughts, as with a flurry of wings, Bob sailed through the air and landed on May's shoulders. The scarlet Macaw glared at her from his perch, dipping his head and playfully biting May's cheek. He didn't take kindly to strangers, as Abi had discovered the previous evening. Her fingers still throbbed from his indignation at being stroked.

'Remind me why you have that creature,' Abi leaned back on her stool, eyeing him warily.

'I told you, sweetie, he turned up one morning when I was having coffee on the balcony. Just flew straight onto the railings and stared at me. And we've been best friends ever since... Haven't we, Bob, who's a good boy?' she cooed at him, scratching his neck with a free hand.

'Me, me!' screeched the bird happily, flapping his brilliantly coloured wings.

'And besides, he's beautiful, and he keeps me company,' she added. 'Despite the... Er, carnage,' she laughed, looking around at the shredded papers scattered across the floor and the lumps hacked out of the door frame. Abi had watched in horror last night as the bird had travelled through the apartment on a voyage of destruction, her aunt seemingly oblivious to his aggression and desire to destroy everything in his path.

Before she could dwell on it further, Aunt May placed a plate of scrambled eggs on toast on the counter in front of her. It was her favourite comfort food since childhood, and she smiled up at her gratefully.

'After lunch, I am supposed to be taking my shift at the protest. I don't know if you fancy coming along?'

'Absolutely,' said Abi, between mouthfuls. 'We can't let those rich fat cats get away with it! I hate these developer types who think they can steamroller over the planet at whim, then bugger off and on to the next project.'

May stood on the other side of the counter, chewing thoughtfully for a few moments before saying quietly, 'not everyone is like your dad, Abi.'

Abi stared at her, years of bitterness towards her father shining out of her eyes. 'I wasn't talking about *him* necessarily. Just these people who want to develop lands that should be left to nature or the people that need them. I am going to get behind this protest 100%, it's something else I can apply my organisational skills to.'

Knowing when it was best to let things lie, May changed the subject but was determined she would have to have a conversation with her niece at some point soon. This deep-seated anger towards her father that she had kept bottled up inside for so long wasn't good for her, and she could see that it tainted her outlook on life. It was time Abi knew the truth.

'Before we go to the exhibition centre, I should show you my latest work, so you know what you're letting yourself in for!' she exclaimed breezily, nodding toward the stairs that led up to her studio. When they had finished eating, they cleared away the breakfast things and Abi followed her chattering aunt up the winding staircase to her studio. Bob circled ahead of them with angry shrieks, as if they were trespassing on his territory, swooping through the door at the top and landing on an easel.

'So, I've been experimenting a little. Using bolder colours and such. It's probably very different from the last work you saw. When was that, do you think?' She paused for breath and looked back at Abi, who was grinning.

'Aunt May, the last time I remember seeing any of your work, I was probably about eight. It was before you moved here, when you still lived next door to mum.'

They shared a look of love and regret at the mention of Lily, before continuing up to the converted loft. The open doorway revealed a wide space that was full of natural light from the skylights that punctuated the ceiling. There were stacks of half-finished canvasses piled carelessly about the room, the finished pieces leaned up or hanging on the walls.

Abi walked around slowly as Bob sat on the easel in the centre of the room, ducking up and down, his eyes following her as she made her way around speechlessly, taking in the paintings lined up along the walls, the bright, bold colours and broad brushstrokes revealing her aunt's love for San Sebastian and the surrounding areas.

'These are fantastic, May,' she whispered in awe, looking around in time to see her aunt's face change from pensive to glee.

'Oh my, I am so glad you like them!' she said earnestly, looking around at them now with pride.

'What's not to like? They're beautiful,' said Abi, exploring further. In the far corner, there were some smaller canvases hung on the wall, and she stopped to examine them. Beaming in delight, she glanced across at May. 'The carousel!' she exclaimed.

The four smaller prints depicted the scene from the same angle but in different seasons. Here flowers were exploding in colourful bloom in pots behind it. In the next one, the beach beyond was packed with tourists enjoying the brilliant sunshine. Next came brown and red autumnal leaves, dancing around the bright colours of the carousel. Finally, a chilly scene, people wrapped up in big coats, scarves and gloves with wind-whipped faces, still looking on with pride as their children beamed on the ride, clutching the poles with their brightly mittened hands.

'Wow, May. I seriously did not know how talented you are. What we need is to make a big splash for your next exhibition. Come on, let's get down there so I can have a look at the gallery.'

As they walked down to the exhibition centre, the streets were bustling with students on their way to college and office workers trailing their way into work, clutching their coffees and croissants like a life-line. The delectable smells wafted across as they scurried past, heads down.

They cut through Christina Enea Park and walked down to Tabakalera, the cultural centre which would host the exhibition. The impressive squat, cream and terracotta building had enormous, arched glass doors, decorated with ironwork fillagree, leading into an airy foyer where you could look up through several levels of the building. Abi was taken aback. She had been expecting a quaint little gallery, down a tiny side street, not this imposing, professional-looking space.

She looked at her aunt with new respect. They must

be fairly confident in her work to agree to host the show. They walked up the glossy, wooden stairwell to the level where May was going to hang her paintings. It was a large, minimalist space with floor to ceiling windows across the far wall that let in the light and an impressive view of the city skyline.

'This is perfect,' said Abi excitedly. 'Your work will look amazing and stand out wonderfully in here. How long do I have to get organised?'

'The exhibition is the first week of May, so we have a couple of weeks,' her aunt smiled nervously. 'I have a list of the emails from the people who came last time, if that helps?'

'Yes, that's a good start. But we should have a big opening on the first night, a party. Get some publicity,' said Abi, getting into work mode and making notes on her phone. 'It would be great if we could invite some local dignitaries, some other artists, preferably local, and maybe a celebrity or two. That would really make the news. Any ideas?'

Aunt May had gone pale and looked a little terrified. 'I... I don't know,' she muttered, fiddling with the beads of her necklace.

Abi took pity on her usually confident aunt. 'Don't worry. I'll do a little research when we get home. Maybe there's someone we can ask. What about that barman, Miquel? He seemed pretty clued up.'

'Oh yes, yes, good idea, and maybe we can ask Pedro,

you know, for an older perspective. He was born and raised here, so I'm sure he will have some ideas.' May beamed, happy she could contribute something to the conversation.

'That's a wonderful start. Seriously.' She turned around, taking in the room's size. 'We are going to need at least a hundred people to fill this place.'

Blanching at the notion, May grabbed her hand. 'Come on then. Let's go to the office. Pedro should be there now. We can ask him about work for you and brainstorm some ideas for the guest list.'

Pedro was not at all what Abi was expecting from her aunt's descriptions of him. She had completely failed to mention how good-looking he was. He looked to be in his early sixties, but his dark hair was only lightly streaked with grey and the stubble around his jawline was decidedly sexy.

His face lit up when he saw May walk through the door of his office, and he immediately jumped up and embraced her.

'Mi corazón,' he said warmly, 'how are you?' he released his grip and pulled back, his dark eyes searching her face.

May looked around, flustered. 'I... I am fine, thank you, Pedro,' she said formally. 'Can I introduce you to my niece, Abigail?'

Finally, seeing there was someone else in the room, he reached out and took her hands in his, smiling in delight as he squeezed them in welcome.

'My, your family produces fine looking women, don't they?' He asked, his eyes glinting in amusement. From anyone else, this would have sounded completely cheesy, but his genuine face, the warm smile and possibly his accent, made it seem like a completely natural complement. Abi flushed slightly, unsure how to respond, and had to look away from his earnest gaze.

'Welcome to San Sebastian,' he said, letting go of her hands and walking back to perch on his desk. 'What are your plans while you are here?'

'That's something I wanted to speak to you about,' May butted in, taking a seat on the well-worn green sofa in the corner. 'Abi is planning to spend the summer here, at least,' she cast a hopeful glance at her niece. 'But we need to find her some work. Do you have any ideas?'

'I am sure we can come up with something,' he replied in an avuncular tone. 'What do you do, Abigail?'

'I was a party planner. You know, organising events, weddings, anything like that, really.'

'Is that so...' he mused, rubbing his chin. 'That seems very fortuitous. May, do you remember that American company I told you about that wants to come and look at some apartments?'

May's brow furrowed. 'Vaguely,' she replied. 'Aren't they some kind of holiday company?'

'Holiday club,' he corrected gently. 'Basically, they charge exorbitant membership fees to guarantee their customers absolute quality wherever they travel with them. They will be here in two days' time to look for an apartment to include in what they call their 'City Breaks' program.'

A glimmer of recognition flickered across May's face. 'Oh yeah, I remember now. You did tell me. You want me to show them the properties we have when they're here. Didn't you say that if the first property sells well with their members, they would be interested in finding another for next year?'

He chuckled, 'I'm glad something about that conversation sank in. And yes, this could be very lucrative for us.'

May had the decency to look a little sheepish, but not for long.

'What has that got to do with Abi?'

'They have asked me to help find a concierge for the apartment. From what I can gather, their members are pretty high maintenance and like to plan everything well in advance. Restaurants, tours, wine tastings. You name it, they want to do it. They have asked us to come up with a list for what they call the "Sublime Week" which is sent out as a suggestion of activities.'

'Well, organisation is my middle name,' chimed Abi.

'But I have never been here before. I know nothing about the city or the area. I'm not sure I would be the best choice for the job.'

'You have a couple of days to explore and come up with some ideas. We will help you, of course, won't we, Pedro?' May asked eagerly.

Abi's mind was racing. This sounded like the perfect opportunity, but would she be up to the task? It appeared to be a big deal for Pedro and his company. The thought of being responsible for the success of this venture was, quite frankly, terrifying. Her insides quaked with the dread of letting him down. Not being good enough for this fancy American company.

'Don't forget, I am helping you to set up your exhibition, Aunt May,' she said. 'That's going to take up a lot of my time...' she trailed off, looking for an escape route. But Aunt May was having none of it. She got up and walked over, gripped her shoulders, and looked determinedly into her eyes.

'Listen to me, Abigail Johnson. You can do anything you set your mind to. You are more like your father than you would ever care to admit and look at how successful he is.' She paused as Abi digested this and carried on before she could argue. 'You also have a strong streak of determination which you got from my dear Lily. You have all the tools you need to knock this out of the park, so don't you be giving me excuses!'

Taken aback at the fierceness emanating from her

aunt, who was visibly vibrating with indignation, Abigail realised she was being defeatist, sinking back into the mire that had kept her from finding a job for the last six months, and that wouldn't do at all. Her decision to come here had been made because she wanted to take back control of her life, start being pro-active and fight against the recent curve balls it had thrown at her.

'You're right, Aunt May,' she admitted. 'Not necessarily that I am like my father, but I am certainly capable of giving this my best shot.'

She smiled at May, then turned to Pedro. 'That reminds me. We were hoping you'd have some contacts we could invite to the opening party for my aunt's art exhibition? Do you know anyone important around here, connected to the media or maybe someone on the council?'

Pedro's handsome face split into a huge grin and he looked at May, shaking his head affectionately. 'Do you ever listen to anything I say?' he teased.

'What do you mean?' asked May, flushing, her bright blue eyes darting away from his gaze.

'I mean like when I told you that my cousin, Alexandro, got the job reporting for El Diario Vasco,' he said, and seeing Abi's confusion added, 'it's the biggest local daily newspaper. Reports everything that is happening around here.' Abigail nodded, smiling. This was a great start to her plan.

'And also, when I took you to that party at City Hall last year?' he continued, looking at May again. 'Why do you think I took you there?'

'Free canapes?' May asked, looking lost.

'No! Although the food was very good. But the reason they invited me was because my other cousin had just been elected mayor of San Sebastian.'

'Pedro, you have about two hundred cousins,' May retorted. 'You can't expect me to keep up with what each and every one of them does with their lives,' she exclaimed defensively.

Laughing affectionately, he stood, going over to give her a quick hug. 'May, I am teasing you. I know full well your head is full of your wonderful paintings, not the goings-on of my extended family.'

Glancing up at the clock on the wall, he declared, 'I think it is lunchtime. What do you say, ladies? Shall we go and celebrate?'

'I'm always ready for more food,' said Abi, 'but what are we celebrating?'

'Life, my dear Abigail, life!' he proclaimed, not taking his eyes off Aunt May.

Abi followed them as they walked out to the street, talking away, and wondered if her aunt realised the depth of feelings this charming man had for her. Probably not, she decided. Her aunt was many wonderful things, but her powers of observation were usually kept for her artwork.

They opted to go back to Baztan Pintxos & Bar, and Miquel greeted them warmly. 'Lovely to see you again so soon, Abi,' he said, handing her a menu with an extended smile before listing the day's specials. When he'd taken their order and bustled off to the kitchen, May said, 'I think our friendly waiter has taken rather a shine to you, Abi.'

Abi snorted. 'I think he's just being an excellent host, Aunt May. He's only just met me.'

'It doesn't mean he couldn't be attracted to you,' Pedro said. 'There is such a thing as love at first sight, you realise,' he added, glancing at May as he took a sip of wine.

Abi could feel herself blushing. 'Well, that's as maybe, but the last thing I am interested in right now is romance. I don't need another man in my life to let me down,' she exclaimed hotly. 'I just want to get on with my life and the job in hand.' She pulled a notebook and pen out of her bag. 'Shall we continue with the guest list?'

'How many do we have now?' asked May a short while later, as their lunch was served. Abi counted up. 'There's twenty so far, which, if you include their plusones, makes forty. That's a great start,' she beamed at them. 'Now, why don't you two give me some ideas about what there is to do around here that you think would appeal to these American tourists?'

They chatted away over their plate of pintxos. Succulent morsels of battered prawns, beef ribs and wonderful fresh artichokes cooked with mushrooms. The flavours were incredible. Abi was completely infatuated with this way of eating. Getting to try out so many different dishes was amazing, and she eagerly sampled each plate.

Miquel came to clear away the dishes when they had finished. 'I couldn't help but overhear your conversation,' he said shyly. 'My sister runs a wine and pintxos tour if you are interested?'

'That sounds perfect,' Abi smiled up at him in delight.

'I have a night off tomorrow,' Miquel continued, 'I could take you if you like? I mean, only if you wanted to, of course,' he stuttered.

'Um,' said Abi, looking to May for support and finding just a knowing grin. 'Ok. That would be very helpful for my work.' she added deliberately, glancing angrily at May, who was sniggering into her beer. They exchanged numbers, and he said he would message her later, after he had spoken with his sister, to let her know what time and where to meet.

A silence fell across the table as he left, the older couple not daring to look at Abi.
'Don't say a word, either of you, not a damn word!'

Gabe was happy to see an email come through from Adam Flynn confirming he would have the first option on the new property in Spain, which was going to be announced by the end of the week. He was less thrilled to see the string of voicemails from Natasha, who, it seemed, wasn't planning to take the break up gracefully. Sighing, he deleted them without listening to them and smoothed down his hair.

'Marianna,' he said into the intercom, 'can you come through? I want to discuss my schedule.'

His assistant sashayed into the room with her usual snake-like grace, which he determinedly ignored. He'd made the mistake before of mixing business with pleasure in the office. It was not an experience he wanted to relive. Shaking that ugly scene from his mind, he looked up at her.

'Run through what I have scheduled from...' he scanned at the calendar on his desk. 'Say, May 7th week?'

She dutifully ran through the extensive list of his appointments for that period, pausing when she got to the end and looking at him expectantly.

'Right, well, I want that week cleared. See if we can bring any of them forward, squeeze them in wherever you can. Otherwise, they will have to wait until I get back.'

'Get back?' she looked at him in confusion. 'Get back from where?'

'I am going on holiday,' he said with an impish smile that nearly detracted her from her surprise.

'Really?' she asked before she could stop herself.

'Yes, really, Marianna. I am allowed, you know.'

'Of course, Sir. It's just in the three and a half years I have worked for you, I have never known you to take time off. For anything. You didn't even stop working when you were rushed into hospital for a ruptured appendix!'

Laughing, because what she had said was entirely true, Gabe realised he was looking forward to the trip. Seeing somewhere new, trying to achieve something different. He was becoming conscious of the fact that his current life bored him. The constant hustle for the next deal, the endless line-up of women he dated. It occurred to him that the thrill of the chase, in both cases, had palled some time ago and he was more than ready for something new.

As he let Marianna return to her office, there was a sinking feeling in his stomach that he couldn't ignore. Becoming successful and independent had been his sole purpose in life since he was a kid. What the hell was he supposed to do now? 'Focus on your next idea, man,' he said to the empty office and opened up the browser on his computer to do exactly that.

Abi and May arrived at the protest in time to swap shifts with the morning group. There was a flurry of introductions and they gave her a placard to hold.

She soon got the hang of the phrase being shouted as they marched around in circles. It was liberating to be doing something so proactive, attracting looks and occasional hoots of support from the passing traffic. She gathered snippets of information about the animals that lived on the land they were fighting for and she pulled up short when May pointed out the orphanage that sat on the far side.

'It would be a shame for those kiddies to lose access to all this land,' her aunt looked out across the expanse of green wistfully. 'It's where they come to play.'

'That's horrible,' Abi replied. Thinking about those poor children having to give up their playground after already losing so much made tears well up in her eyes. She started marching determinedly round again, shouting as loud as she could, her mind working on plausible ideas to help the cause. She would stop these dastardly property developers if it was the last thing she did.

CHAPTER FOUR

From: Adamflynn@sublimeretreats.com

To: PedroZubiri@donostiaestates.es

Subject: San Sebastian Acquisition Schedule

Good morning, Pedro,

We are looking forward to meeting you tomorrow.

Thank you for arranging the car to pick us up at the airport. We will go straight to the hotel, drop our bags, and be ready to meet your colleague at 2 pm, all being well.

The list of properties you sent looks very interesting. Can we focus on the ones with sea views? They would certainly have the most appeal for our members.

Many thanks,

Adam

Adam Flynn

Acquisitions Manager

Sublime Retreats

Abigail climbed up to the studio, where her aunt was painting, to say goodbye to her before going to meet Miquel.

'I'll see you later, Aunt May,' she called from the doorway, warily watching Bob. 'I won't be late, I don't think.'

'Is that what you're wearing?' she asked, putting down her brush and gazing at Abi's jeans and t-shirt with disdain. Her face was smudged with dark red paint and another brush was behind her ear, staining her silver hair orange. 'You could make a little effort for your date.' May absently put out her arm as Bob announced his intent and flew from his perch in the corner where he had been preoccupied with ripping up a newspaper, and landed protectively on her, glaring at Abi's intrusion.

'It is not a date,' she retorted, pulling a hairband out of her pocket and furiously binding her long red hair into a ponytail. 'I am simply meeting someone who has kindly offered to help me find a tour for these Americans. That's all!'

'If you say so,' her aunt grinned infuriatingly, stroking Bob's head. 'Wouldn't do you any harm to have some fun in the process, though.'

'Fun, fun!' echoed the bird, bobbing up and down in glee.

Smiling at her aunt, Abi replied, 'I appreciate the sentiment, May. But as I said before, I am sick and tired of being let down by men. Miquel seems like a nice enough guy; I hope we can become friends.'

'He is nice. And dependable. Seems just your type.'

'Dependable is what landed me here,' Abi replied shortly, thinking of easy-going, apparently reliable Jason. 'Not that I'm not happy to be here,' she blurted. 'I am just determined to be in control from now on. You know, actually take part in life, rather than just reacting to what happens to me. That includes, when it happens, choosing who I date, not just falling into a relationship with the first person who asks me out. I did that with Jason and I understand now that it was just an easy option, not passion.'

Nodding in understanding, May said, 'well that sounds like a fine way to be. Don't ignore some possibilities because they're too easy, though. You never know what's right under your nose.'

'You're a fine one to talk!' escaped from Abi's mouth before she could censor it. 'I have to go,' she said quickly, before May could utter the question that was forming on her lips. 'See you later!' she called as she hastened down the stairs. Abi wasn't sure what was going on with her aunt and Pedro, but now wasn't the time to talk about it. She had a meeting to get to.

She had arranged to meet Miquel by the carousel, as it was the only place in town she knew with any certainty. As she walked towards the seafront, she was beset by doubts again, niggling away at her insecurities. Sublime Retreats. She had looked at their website. Well, as much as she could, you had to be a member to access most of it. It was a high-end company that would have high-end guests. 'Members, Abi, members', she corrected herself as she hurried along, ignoring the startled glance from the old lady walking her poodle in the opposite direction. Was she really good enough to work for such a fancy company with their monied members? She was so worried about getting something wrong, she could barely think straight.

Approaching the carousel, she spotted Miquel leaning against a tree, watching it twirl with a smile on his face. She gave a little wave when he looked up and spotted her. His smile broadened, and he pushed off the tree to come and meet her.

'Hi, Abi, I am so glad you came.' He gazed down at her. Abi shifted her position, so she was looking back at the carousel, and said with a nod in its direction, 'I gather you like that as much as my aunt and I do?'

'Sí,' he confirmed, still smiling. 'Everyone loves it. I used to beg my parents to let me ride it when I was a boy.'

'I can imagine,' she said with a wry smile, picturing a tiny Miquel imploring his parents for yet another spin.

'Your aunt probably likes the paintings on the ceiling,' he added. Seeing her furrowed brow, he took her elbow and walked them closer to the spinning carousel and pointed up. It took a moment to register, but then Abigail made sense of what she was seeing. The ceiling had pictures evenly spaced around it, images representing what must be famous paintings. She recognised Van Gogh's Sunflowers before she saw his name carefully written underneath.

The ride was slowing down, much to the disappointment of the children on it, and she took the opportunity to take some pictures with her phone, thinking she could research the paintings and artists to tell her guests about them.

'I had a thought to do a brief walking tour with these Americans when they come,' she said, snapping away, angling her phone to get the best shots. 'You know, a kind of orientation on their first day?'

'That's a good idea,' he responded. 'It gives you a chance to get to know them a little, which will probably make the week easier.'

'That was my thinking. I want them to feel comfortable with me, so they can ask for anything.' She glanced up at him, biting her lower lip in concern.

He looked at her. 'You're a bit stressed out by this job, aren't you?'

Mortified that her self-doubt was so painfully clear,

even to a complete stranger, Abi remained mute. Staring unfocused at the flashing lights, she felt a light pressure as he reached out and squeezed her shoulder.

'Don't overthink it, is my advice,' he said gently. 'These people know even less about San Sebastian than you do, so you will be ahead of the game.'

She laughed, 'you're right, Miquel. I could actually just make stuff up and they would have no idea!'

He joined in her laughter. 'Exactly, but let's make sure you know some truths before they arrive. Come, let's go and meet my sister.'

Miquel's sister was waiting for them outside a small bar in a part of the old town that Abi hadn't seen before. Anya was delightful, easy to talk to, a mine of local information and looked exactly like Miquel, just with longer hair. She was extremely pretty with olive skin and dark hair and had the same easy-going smile. They sat at a table outside, as it was a mild evening, and she explained what the tour usually involved. 'I take them around six different bars, all with excellent pintxos, and they get to try various local wines along the way,' she smiled.

'Would there be other people on the tour?' asked Abi, making notes on her pad.

'Never,' Anya replied. 'It is a private tour, completely curated for your guests. I know not everyone likes to eat the same foods or wants to hear about Basque's history. A lot of the women want to know where to shop, and their men want to know which bar they can wait for them in,' she laughed.

'I have to say, this sounds perfect,' Abi said, feeling a sense of achievement for the first time in ages.

'Would you like us to visit a couple of them? So you can see where we go?' Anya looked at her.

Abi considered this for a moment, then shook her head. 'You know, what I would like to do is pick your brains a little more.' Seeing twin looks of confusion across the table, she explained. 'I need more ideas of things to do around here and to get to know some history about the place?'

Before she knew it, three hours had passed. She looked at the time in disbelief. Her notepad was full of ideas, and Anya, who it turned out was a bit of a local influencer, had enthusiastically agreed to post about aunt May's art exhibition on her Instagram feed. Abi felt content as she walked back to her aunt's home, gallantly chaperoned by Miquel. There was an awkward pause when they reached the gate. Abi looked up at the lights glowing from her aunt's windows, sanctuary beckoning.

'So, Miquel. Thank you for this evening. I had a great time.' She looked at him and saw he was staring at her with a peculiar look of concentration on his face that made her insides squirm. Quickly rummaging in her bag for her keys, she hoped he would take the hint.

'I had a good time too, Abi,' he replied huskily. 'In

fact, I was hoping we could do this again sometime soon?'

'Look, Miquel, I really enjoyed your company and I would be happy to do this again. But you must know I see you as a friend, nothing more, if we're going to hang out.' His puppy dog expression made her heart sink, but she knew it was only fair to be honest. He was far too nice to be strung along.

'Of course, of course,' he murmured, 'that's fine,' he lied with a small, brave smile.

Feeling guilty as hell, she said goodnight and walked up the stairs to the apartment. She could hear her aunt singing as she opened the door.

'Hi, Abi, how was it?' she called when she saw her.

'It was a great evening, May. I just feel a little bad for Miquel. You were right. He thought that this was a date.'

Seeing her niece's distraught face, May pulled her down onto the sofa and told her, 'Abi, that is not anything you should feel guilty about. Although it was patently clear to anybody with a set of eyes in their head,' she couldn't help adding. 'It's not your fault he was harking up the wrong tree!'

Laughing, Abi hugged her aunt. 'You're right. I made it pretty clear from the start, and again just now. So hopefully we can move forward and be friends.'

'Hmm, I'm not sure that will work. But you never know. He's a sensible lad, he may be able to cope with being in the friend-zone.'

The next day, May was due to meet the people from Sublime Retreats to show them the potential apartments. She left early to have a meeting with Pedro beforehand, leaving Abi alone with her thoughts. Not wanting to dwell on the train wreck that was her life, she worked on designing the invitation email for the exhibition. The email list for the opening night was growing by the day, giving her hope that the event wouldn't be a complete flop.

When she'd been the only person 'let go' from Polished Events last year, her confidence had sunk to rock bottom. Abigail had made all the right noises at the time. Of course, she understood, and yes, she was sure she would find something else soon enough. And she had tried, tentatively sending out her CV to a few companies, but nobody was hiring in the industry, and each rejection she received dragged her further into a mire of depression that left her unable to get out of bed on some days.

Jason would come home from work to find her slobbing on the sofa, binge-watching on Netflix, still in her pyjamas. When he started coming home later and later and became quiet and morose around the flat, she had just presumed it was in direct response to her foul mood.

Abigail caught herself gazing out of the window,

lost in the events of the last year, and pulled herself back into the present. 'Focus on the now, girl,' she said to the empty room and then giggled. She was beginning to sound like her aunt. When her stomach growled, she realised it was already lunchtime. She was finally happy with the design for the invitation, so she went to investigate the contents of the fridge. Throwing together a salad with some left-over chicken, she mused over what she should wear this evening.

They were having dinner with the Sublime Retreats managers. Pedro had assured her it wasn't an interview; they were taking his word for her suitability as a concierge. But doubts flitted around her head, no matter how hard she batted them away. Polished Events had cast her aside without a second thought after ten years. Why should this company feel any more confident about her?

Her stomach baulked, and she covered the rest of her lunch in clingfilm and put it in the fridge. She decided to take a walk to clear her head and soak up some local atmosphere. Maybe that would boost her confidence a little. By the time she got back to the apartment, she had rid herself of most of her doubts, well squirrelled them away in a corner of her mind at least, and got ready to go and meet them.

It appeared that any worries she'd had about the meeting were unfounded. Peter from Sublime Retreats turned out to be charming and seemed to love the list of ideas she had found for the Sublime Week.

Adam, who was incredibly good looking, but seemed a little distant and distracted, was harder to read. Over a wonderful meal of Txuleta steaks and with a side of Patatas bravas topped with creamy aioli and a fiery tomato sauce, they explained a little how the company worked and what they expected of her, as the concierge.

'So, Abi,' Peter smiled at her across the table. 'You will basically be on call 24/7 for our members.' Seeing her horrified expression, he laughed. 'Don't worry. Most of them are pretty self-sufficient, but there are some that need their hands held the entire time. You'll soon get the hang of it.' Adam's phone rang, and he stood up quickly, his chair almost tipping over in his haste. 'Excuse me, I have to take this,' he said before scurrying outside.

'You'll have to excuse my colleague. He and his wife Sofia just had a baby and I think he's finding it tough being away from them.'

That would explain it, reflected Abi, relief flooding through her that his attitude wasn't anything to do with her. Sure enough, when he came back in, he was all smiles and it didn't take much to convince him to show her the endless gallery of photos he had of his baby girl.

Within a few days, she had her own SR email set up and was bombarded with information on how the club ran and what the members expected. Which was basically everything as far as she could see. There were a couple of early morning Zoom sessions to walk her through the Dashboard, the system that contained all the information gathered about club members. Likes, dislikes, divorces, kids, preferred chocolate, you name it; the system had minutiae of these people's lives. It felt a bit like stalking to Abi, but she realised it would come in handy when suggesting and setting up their itineraries.

When she wasn't learning what she could about her new job, Abi was working on the art exhibition that was rapidly approaching. So far, the response to her invitations had been positive, and her idea to include a line where they could suggest other people who would enjoy the event had proved an excellent one, providing her with a whole host of other guests to invite. They were running adverts in the local papers and Anya had uploaded pictures of some of May's paintings to her Instagram, which were garnering a lot of response.

A week before the big event, she had sent her first introductory email to the first member that was due in resort the day after the party.

'You'll find this one an exception to the rule, Abi,' Adam had told her when she had queried the lack of information about him on the Dashboard. All it said was he had to have excellent coffee available in large quantities. 'He usually only travels for work and everything he does goes through his assistant. Don't expect anything but the bare minimum of travel information. He's a bit of a lone wolf.'

Determined to wow this Gabe Xavier, she had emailed his assistant and waited eagerly for a reply, constantly checking her inbox, in case she had missed a notification. One of the many rules with SR was that she had to respond to emails within 24 hours, and she didn't want to fail at the first hurdle. When the reply finally came, it was brief. All it just said was that he would arrive by private jet, no times as yet, and would make his own way to the apartment. No requests, no interest in the Sublime Week suggestions. Nothing she could get her teeth into and organise. She blew through pursed lips, causing aunt May to glance up from her seat at the kitchen counter.

'What's up?' she asked, seeing the frown on Abi's face.

'This guy, Gabe Xavier. His assistant has emailed me but it doesn't sound like she knows what he wants any more than I do,' she sighed. May came around and read the email over her shoulder.

'Nope, there's not much info there,' she chortled. 'Sounds like a bit of a stark horse, this one, and no mistake. Would you like some coffee?' she asked as she went to fill the water compartment of the machine.

'Yes please, May. I don't know how I am supposed to organise things for him if he doesn't tell me what he wants,' Abi moaned.

Turning back to face her, May said, 'don't stress it, Abi. When he arrives, you can see what's needed. This early in the season, it shouldn't be difficult to get him in wherever he wants to go. Who is he bringing with him?'

'I don't know!' Abi sounded exasperated. 'I don't bloody know anything.' She slapped her laptop shut and glared at May, who giggled.

'Oh my, you do look like Lily when you're angry,' she sniggered. Unable to stop it, Abi felt a smile stretch over her face. The mention of her mum calmed her instantly, and she said, 'you're right. I will have to deal with him when he arrives on Saturday. In the meantime, we need to decide what you are wearing to the opening night on Friday.'

Standing up and holding out her palm to stop her aunt from replying, she added, 'you are not wearing a kaftan!'

Crestfallen, May said, 'well what do you have in mind?'

'We are going to go shopping,' Abi replied with a glint in her eyes, determined to glam May up a bit for such an important event.

'Well, if I have to get something new, so do you,' she answered, equally determinedly, glaring at her.

'I don't have the funds for a new outfit yet, May. I won't get paid until the end of the month.'

'Don't you worry about that. Call it a thank you

from me for all the hard work you've put in organising this. I would have been lost without you.'

'You don't need to thank me, May,' she cried. 'You've done so much for me already. I can't possibly accept.'

'If you don't get a new outfit for the exhibition, then neither will I!' she retorted triumphantly. 'It's my way on the highway.' And that, it seemed, was that.

CHAPTER FIVE

To: abigailjohnson@sublimeretreats.com

From: office@xavierindustries.com

Subject: San Sebastian Trip

Dear Ms Johnson,

In response to your follow up email, I am afraid I still do not have the timings for Mr Xavier's flight. I have been unable to reach him in the last 24 hours, which is not unusual, but if he comes back to me with his plans, I will, of course, let you know.

I have advised him that he can check in to the property from 2 pm onwards on Saturday and I have given him your cell number in case of any difficulties.

Best regards,

Marianna

Executive Assistant

Xavier Industries

Abi stood gazing at her reflection in the full-length mirror in her bedroom, hardly recognising the woman standing there. The shimmering emerald dress embraced her curves perfectly, dropping to just above her knees. The colour offset her red hair, which she'd tamed with some effort into a chignon, and it brought out the green in her recently lacklustre hazel eyes. Her aunt knocked and walked in, gasping when Abi turned round.

'You look beautiful. I told you that dress was perfect for you. I have an eye for these things, you know.'

'Thank you for making me get this one,' Abi said, glad she had given in to her aunt's insistence. 'It's not something I would usually choose, but I feel so like Cinderella right now.'

Aunt May beamed. She was looking pretty classy herself. She had chosen a fitted black velvet dress with capped sleeves and had a vivid purple wrap draped around her shoulders which complemented her inevitable beads, strung in rows around her neck.

Hearing the toot of the horn of the car Pedro had insisted on hiring for the occasion, she crooked an arm. 'Shall we go to the ball, Cinderella?' she enquired with an excited smile.

Laughing, Abi linked her arm through hers. 'I think

we should, but remember, this is your big night. Any Prince Charmings that are there, we want them to buy paintings, not chase around with glass slippers!' Laughing, the pair of them made their way down to the waiting car.

It wasn't long before the party was in full swing. The room that had seemed so large before crowded with guests now, and the sound of excited chattering and clinking champagne flutes competed with the four-piece ensemble playing discreetly in one corner. An openly admiring Pedro had whisked Aunt May away as soon as they arrived to meet some of the more important guests. Abi snatched up a glass of champagne from a passing waiter and wandered around the room, looking for familiar faces.

She was delighted by the turnout and amazed yet again by her aunt's paintings. They looked even more wonderful now, hung in this incredible space. As she explored the room, she could see there were already a few with red dots on them. It seemed safe to say that this, the first event she had planned in so long, was going to be a success. Smiling, she stopped in front of the four smaller paintings of the carousel that had grabbed her attention before. Lost in admiration, she was only partially aware of another guest coming and standing just behind her.

'They are enchanting, aren't they?' said a deep, male voice at her shoulder. Turning to agree with him, she came face to chest with the stranger, and as she looked up to his face, she caught a hint of his cedar cologne.

Abi gulped. Standing painfully close was the best-looking man she had ever laid eyes on. He was tall and his broad frame was ensconced in what looked to be a very expensive, deep blue suit that matched his brooding eyes. She had never seen such a dark blue. They were almost navy. He smiled, and a dimple appeared on his left cheek, amusement playing across his face and raw sexuality exuding from him in waves.

Abi realised she was gawping, so took a step back, glancing at the paintings to hide the blush creeping up her neck.

'Yes. Yes, they are,' she managed, with just a glance behind. Yup, he was still standing too close and yup, still gorgeous.

Taking a step forward, as if to examine the artwork more closely, she moved out of range of whatever pheromones he was emitting, hoping he would move along swiftly to look at something else.

'Do you know anything about the artist?' he asked, squashing her hopes of some time to get her act together, his voice resonating through her like a plucked cello string.

'I do, she's my aunt as it happens,' Abi replied, looking around the room until she spotted May and pointing to her. 'There she is over there,' she said, just as May let out a raucous laugh that could be heard across the room, at something Pedro had whispered in her ear.

'She certainly seems to be enjoying herself,' he said

bitingly, and she looked up at him again. There was a smirk on his face now as he watched aunt May, and she bristled.

'She's allowed to! This is her special night, the culmination of years of work,' she snapped. 'If you'll excuse me, I have to go and... go and do something.'

She stalked off as fast as her new high heels would allow, conscious of his eyes on her behind as she walked away. Her blood still thrumming and rattled by the encounter, she cast about until she spotted Miquel and Anya with a group of friends near the bar and made a beeline for them.

Miquel lit up when he saw her, and she had a rush of gratitude at his familiar face and welcoming smile.

'Hi, Abi,' said Anya, coming over to kiss her cheeks. 'I hope you are enjoying the party?' she asked.

'I was,' Abi replied with a frown, casting around for the annoying, if handsome, stranger, but not finding him.

'Is everything OK?' her friend asked, looking with concern at her flushed cheeks. Not able to explain what had just happened even to herself, let alone anyone else, Abi just nodded. 'Yes, everything is fine. It's a fantastic turnout. Thank you so much for all your help, both of you,' she smiled at the siblings.

Putting the stranger out of her mind, she continued to mingle. She dragged May away from Pedro, much to his disappointment, to chat to some of the other guests about her work. They did the rounds of the room and then did them again, stopping off to talk to anyone looking interested in the artwork and a couple of people interested in commissioning May for special projects. Abi could see some more paintings had sold by the time she finally allowed their aching feet to rest on a bar stool. They sat, sipping champagne and people-watching as the evening wound down.

Aunt May burped, then downed another glass of champagne with gusto. 'This has been amazing, Abi,' she enthused. 'I don't know why I didn't think of asking for your help before.'

'We Johnson women are not very good at asking for help,' Abi replied, thinking of her own inability to do so. How long had it taken her to get up the courage to call May last month?

May cackled. 'We all have our bears to cross,' she said with a hiccup, and grabbed another glass. Abi decided it was time to get the star of the evening home before she imbibed any more and went to find Pedro to ask him to organise the car home.

She felt the man's gaze on her before she saw him lounging against a column, his eyes boring into her. Warmth flooded her neckline again, and she saw that dimple reappear as he raised an eyebrow at her. 'Who the hell is that guy?' she muttered, spinning around, almost tripping over in her haste, but thankfully keeping her balance as she saw Pedro just ahead through the crowd and hurried across.

'Sorry to interrupt,' she said, nodding at his companion. 'Pedro, I think it's time I got May home. Could you call the driver, please?'

'Of course, *Mijita.* I will call him now,' he replied and pulled his phone from his pocket. A short conversation later and he said, 'OK, he is on his way. He will meet you outside in a few minutes.'

'Thank you, Pedro,' she said fervently and scurried back to the bar, keeping her eyes fixed straight ahead and hoping Aunt May hadn't found any more champagne. Her hopes were dashed when she heard May's warbling tones singing "It's My Party and I'll Cry if I Want to", at the top of her voice. Wincing, Abi strode over, took the glass from her inebriated aunt and pulled her wrap, which had slipped to the floor, back around her shoulders.

'Come on, May,' she cajoled, 'time to wrap this up and get you home.'

'But I don't want to go home. I'm having a thoroughly lovely time,' her aunt replied petulantly.

Thankful that the irritating man was nowhere to be seen and not witnessing this, Abi said, 'please, May. For me? You know I have the first arrival at the apartment tomorrow. I need to get some sleep, it's practically midnight.'

This seemed to register. Her aunt's face grew serious for a moment. 'Are you going to turn into a pumpkin?' she howled in delight, slapping at her thighs and missing. Grinning, Abi lifted her up and, under the guise of supporting her, firmly steered her towards the door.

She eventually poured the old woman into the car and got her back to the apartment, staggering up the stairs with effort. Convincing her to undress proved to be impossible, so Abi just slipped off her shoes and tucked her up in bed. Placing a glass of water and a packet of paracetamol on the bedside table, she paused in the doorway and looked at May's sleeping face. She looked so innocent when she was asleep. She grinned to herself, then having another thought, went into the kitchen and grabbed a large plastic bowl to leave next to the bed. Just in case.

Saturday morning arrived with a bang. The sound of shattering glass roused Abi from a deep sleep and she lay there groggily for a few minutes, trying to remember where she was. The voice of her aunt cursing vehemently, accompanied by annoyed shrieks from Bob, brought her memory flooding back and a smile to her face. She threw back the covers, pulled her rose-coloured robe on and cinched the ties. Padding into the kitchen, she saw Aunt May futilely trying to sweep up a smashed bowl, groaning with the effort.

She walked across and smoothly removed the dustpan and brush from her aunt's unresisting hands.

'I've got this, May.'

Nodding, she winced and leaned against the counter, looking deathly pale and shaky.

'Did you take the paracetamol I left out for you?'

May started to nod and winced, then opted for speech instead, her voice a croaky, frog-like affair. 'I wanted to make you breakfast,' she said, shuffling across to the sofa and dropping onto it dramatically. 'But my hand to eye coordination seems to be a little off.'

Laughing, Abi bent to clean up the mess. 'I'm not surprised. You certainly seemed to enjoy yourself last night.' Her words brought back the image of the handsome stranger. Those intense eyes, that knowing look, the dimple. Her stomach flipped alarmingly at the memory of him.

'I was, I did. It was a fantastic start to my exhibition,' May said weakly. 'Thank you, Abi.'

Standing up straight to put the remains of the bowl in the bin, Abi smiled over at her. 'How about I make us some coffee first and then the breakfast?'

'Coffee, desperately. Breakfast? Well, I'll just have to cross that fridge when I get to it.'

Chuckling to herself, Abi set about preparing the coffee. 'Here you go,' she said a short while later, placing the steaming cup on the table. Aunt May pushed herself into a sitting position, looking whey-faced, and stretched a shaky hand out. After a few sips, she seemed to regain some of her usual spark.

'So, today's the big day, huh? First arrival for Sublime Retreats. Are you looking forward to it?'

'I am,' Abi replied. 'I mean, I wish I was more prepared, but I'm excited to start.'

'Prepared?' May scoffed, taking another swig. 'Look
what you managed to do in such a short period of time
for my exhibition. There were loads of people there,
and if I recall, I sold quite a few paintings, although
that could be the champagne remembering.'

Grinning, Abi replied, 'it was pretty good, wasn't
it?', feeling a rush of pride that something she had organised had gone right. 'Talking of the people there,
do you know who that man was? He was tall, much
taller than me, and good-looking if you like that kind
of thing...' she trailed off under the scrutinising look
of her aunt.

'Hey, hey. Someone piqued your interest did they
love?'

'Definitely not, Aunt May,' she protested. 'He was
just a little unusual is all, and I wondered who he was.'

'Unusual is interesting, Abi, and I haven't seen you
even flicker a glance towards a man since you arrived.'

'I'm not interested in men at the moment, May,' Abi
replied emphatically. 'All they do is let you down. And
I'm certainly not interested in Mr Unusual. He was a
bit of a jerk, actually.'

'The best ones generally are,' said May absently, still
examining Abi's face thoughtfully.

Abi jumped up to escape her aunt's scrutinisation.
'I'll start on breakfast. Scrambled eggs?' May tried an-

other nod and, finding it less painful than before, smiled.

'Yes, please.'

As Abi got busy in the kitchen, she tried to put images of Mr Unusual out of her mind, whisking the eggs with fervour, taking her feelings out on them. *I don't need a man*; she thought to herself as she beat viciously. *The last thing I need at the moment is romance. I need to sort myself out, focus on work, make a success of myself. I certainly don't need an arrogant jerk like him.*

'I think those eggs have submitted, Abi,' her aunt called across. Stopping mid-whisk, Abi looked down at the completely beaten contents of the bowl and brought her attention back to the present. Thinking about the handsome stranger wasn't going to get the job done, was it?

CHAPTER SIX

After breakfast was done and dusted, Abi had a shower and got ready to go to the Sublime Retreats apartment. She had spent some time there, despite being so busy in this last week, but she wanted to have a little extra time to familiarise herself with every aspect. She didn't want to be caught short when her first guest asked questions about the place.

With butterflies unsettling her scrambled eggs, she got dressed and tamed her fiery red hair into a ponytail. She glanced in the full-length mirror briefly, before walking back through to the lounge.

'Right, Aunt May. I'm ready as I'll ever be. Is there anything you need before I go?'

May looked up from her iPad. 'You look fantastic, darling. Very professional.' Abi squirmed a little in her blue trouser suit, which was feeling a little tight. She must have put weight on since she'd arrived in Spain. She could barely close the buttons over her breasts. It was always the first-place weight went to, and the last place that needed any help, she thought with a sigh.

Kissing her aunt, she picked up her bag containing all her paperwork and strode out the door. She made her way towards the seafront where the apartment was located, walking over Maria Kristina Zubia, the bridge that allowed her to cross the Urumea river. She stopped halfway, taking a moment to admire the views and making a closer inspection of the statues that spanned the bridge. The sun was brilliant against the backdrop of the blue sky, causing the ripples in the river to shimmer.

Abi knew admiring the view was just a distraction technique, avoiding the moment when her job would begin for real. She was so nervous about mucking things up; she was shaking at the idea. If this didn't go well, God knows what she would do. She was feeling disconnected from her real life as it was.

As much as she was enjoying her time here in Spain, a part of her was secretly worrying about where she was going in the world. She was thirty, for God's sake. She was a grownup. Shouldn't she be settled by now, know where her life was headed? She shook her head as she walked on. For now, she would focus on putting one foot in front of another, everything else she would worry about later.

A passer-by jostled her out of her reverie. 'Barkatu,' the young woman called over her shoulder as she hurried on in front of her. Taking it as a sign to get a move on, Abi followed the woman's path and crossed the bridge, arriving into the old town and following

Boulevard Avenue down to its end where the sea was sparkling in the early morning sunlight. She took a moment and a deep breath of briny air, finding herself smiling as she turned the corner and walked along to the entrance of the apartment. It had delighted her to learn that Sublime Retreats had chosen one that overlooked the carousel and was so close to La Concha Beach; it was the perfect location.

She opened the main door after a couple of tries with the unfamiliar set of keys and walked up the grand marble staircase to the front door of El Carrusel, the name Sublime Retreats had assigned to the property. Letting herself in, she walked over to the windows and pressed the button to lift the electric shutters that were blocking out the light and the view. Sunlight flooded in, breathing life into the space, and she looked around the large living room with a smile. It was beautiful. The style was a little modern for her tastes, but the overall effect was stunning, and as she checked each room in turn, she found the maid had prepared everything perfectly and it was looking spotless.

Going back into the lounge, she picked up her bag and took out the laminated sheets she had prepared with instructions for everything she could think of. From how to use the cooker and the TV to safety instructions, lists of emergency numbers and, of course, her contact details. Next came the checklist that Peter Williams had sent her. Apparently, it was one he had made when he was a lowly concierge in Corfu and was now used as standard across the company.

She walked around the apartment again, conscientiously ticking off every point on the list. She was going to make sure that this Mr Xavier found nothing to complain about. As it was her first guest, she felt it ultra-important that everything should go well and show Sublime Retreats they had good reason to trust Pedro's judgement in employing her. The thought of messing this up sent another flash of panic through her. It didn't bear thinking about.

At that moment, a message pinged through from Miquel, wishing her luck on her first day. He was very sweet; she reflected as she finished her checks. Maybe she should give him a chance and not tar him with the same brush as the previous men in her life, she mused as she came back into the lounge. Seeing that it was one o'clock, and that she had an hour before her first guest could check-in, she went downstairs to have a coffee while she waited.

She sat at the little café that was just a few doors down from the apartment and relaxed a little, letting the warmth of the sun ease her concerns for a moment. She checked her emails. Still no confirmation from Mr Xavier's assistant as to his travel plans. He must be a nightmare to work for, Abi realised. At least I only have to put up with him for a week, she grinned to herself. She drank the last of her coffee and went back up to the apartment. She was still early, but she had brought her Kindle with her so she could read while she waited, as she had no idea how long he would be.

Mounting the stairs, she heard a voice. One side of what sounded like a telephone conversation. As she rounded the corner, she stopped in her tracks. There, leaning nonchalantly against the wall, was Mr Unusual with a carry-on bag by his feet. His eyes met hers, a spark of recognition flashing through them, but he continued talking without faltering. Abi's heart was pounding, her brain racing. No, no, no, it couldn't be. The universe couldn't be that cruel, surely?

The universe apparently could. As he closed the conversation and tucked his phone in his pocket, he smiled at her.

'Abigail Johnson, I presume? What a small world.'

Her legs felt like jelly, but she stood up, straightening her shoulders, levelly meeting his gaze. His eyes flew to her chest as it strained against her jacket.

'Mr Xavier, I presume?' she responded as evenly as she could. 'I would welcome you to San Sebastian, but you have been here a while, it would seem.'

Laughing, he said, 'Indeed. I decided to come early and scope things out. I couldn't wait to see what pleasures awaited me here.' The look on his face was enough to cause her to flush a deep red and Abi had to take a breath. Trying to put the picture of what pleasures with him would be like out of her mind, she bustled efficiently, pulling the keys from her pocket and opening the door of the apartment with a flourish.

'Well, welcome to El Carrusel, then,' she announced, trying desperately to recall the welcome speech she had prepared so carefully, but her brain refused to co-operate.

'Nice recovery,' he smirked knowingly and stalked into the room like a lion assessing danger, dropping his bag casually on the sofa. He stopped in front of the picture window and looked down at the carousel.
'I see why your aunt found the need to paint it,' he said, glancing back at her briefly. Abi gazed at his broad back, tapering down to what she could only describe as a peach of a butt, and tried to make her brain work. It felt fizzy and was being rebellious. Her mouth was dry and her stomach was a hive of disturbing activity.

'Shall I show you the rest of the apartment?' she squeaked. She cleared her throat and then tried again. 'If you'd like to follow me?' and turned on her heel without waiting to see if he followed. She stopped in the kitchen, ready now with her speech on its facilities.

'So, in here we have everything you could need, should you decide to prepare a meal...' she began, but trailed off. He was standing next to her. Too close. She could smell that cedar scent and feel his pulsing presence. Her mouth dried up again, her eyes darting around the room, finally alighting on the coffee machine.

'You will be glad to see we have catered for your

coffee addiction,' she smiled up at him. He was so tall, he must be at least six foot five, she guessed. He smiled that smile, the cute dimple playing unfairly across his cheek again as he stared down at her with that unwavering gaze, his dark eyes giving nothing away.

'I'm glad you're seeing to my addictions, Abigail,' he said in a husky voice that caused shivers to run across her skin and the hairs on her arms to stand to attention.

Caught up in his look, Abi couldn't move, or speak for that matter. Her brain was flashing as her instincts screamed, 'flight, flight!' Rallying her brain and remembering that this was an important day in her current career, she dragged her eyes away with an effort and moved swiftly to the doorway, faltering for just a moment as she realised it led to the bedroom, before moving into the room.

'In here is the master suite with its ensuite bathroom,' she prattled on as if her body was not a whirlpool of molten lava. He moved past her, his elbow brushing across the front of her suit, leaving a trace of awareness, gave the room a cursory glance, and nodded.

'This will do,' he smiled at her. 'Can we talk about what I need to do while I'm here?'

Flustered, Abi said, 'there's still two more bedrooms for you to see.'

'No need. There's only me, I'm sure one bed will

suffice,' he grinned wickedly.

Abi's treacherous mind couldn't help but imagine him in that bed, naked and waiting for her. Shaking the image away, *what the hell is wrong with me*? In a desperate attempt to take control of the situation, she said, 'OK, if we go back into the lounge, I can run through the list of attractions here in San Sebastian.'

She hurried back through and snatched up the paperwork from her bag, holding it in front of her like a shield. He sauntered in after her, seemingly unperturbed, and sat casually on the sofa, arm resting on his bag, looking at her expectantly.

'So, Mr Xavier, did you look at the email I sent through with the suggestions for the Sublime Week?'

He laughed derisively. 'No, Abigail, I did not. And call me Gabe, please.'

She walked over and handed him the printout. 'Well, Gabe,' she gave a tight smile. 'I didn't think you had, so here is a copy. If you want to have a quick look through and let me know if there is anything that grabs your fancy?' His eyes slid down her body and she squirmed. Damn her runaway mouth. She really would have to think twice before she spoke with this man.

Abi walked over to the window and cast a quick look outside. Freedom beckoned, and she felt the need to get out of here as quickly as possible. Remove herself from the presence of Gabe Xavier before she said or did anything else stupid.

'I can recommend the pintxo and wine tour, and there is a lovely private tour of the coastline and its villages,' she finished lamely. It was impossible to imagine this man wanting to do such mundane things. He was still staring at her, and she shifted uncomfortably. Why did he have to be so strange? Her mind railed, her first guest and he was impossible to read, let alone suggest an itinerary for.

He put the paper to one side on the sofa, without even looking at it.

'Actually, Abigail, what I would like to do is take the children from the orphanage just outside of town out for the day.'

Blindsided, she looked at him uncomprehendingly for a moment. She had not been expecting that!

'I want to arrange a minibus to pick them up and take them into town. I want to take them shopping for, I don't know, shoes or whatever. They can pick what they like. And then somewhere for lunch?' He stood and came and stood next to her, looking out and down to the beach in the distance. 'Yes, lunch somewhere by the beach would be perfect. They can run around and get some sea air in their lungs.'

'Erm, well, ok,' she said, brain racing. 'I will have to speak to whoever is in charge over there and see if it's possible, of course.'

'I hardly think they are going to turn it down,' he

smirked. 'Invite the staff, too. They won't want to miss a free lunch.'

God, he was arrogant; she fumed internally as she took a notepad from her bag and started scribbling his ideas down. 'OK, I'll get on it,' she said, looking up at him. 'What's the budget?'

He threw his head back and laughed out loud, as if the idea was completely ridiculous.

'No budget, Abigail dear. Just organise it and I will pay.'

Heat rose and she could feel her face infusing with blood. She was barely controlling the anger she felt towards this insufferable, egotistic jerk who was used to getting his own way.

'Fine. I'll see what I can do, but it will probably take a couple of days. In the meantime?' she enquired as sweetly as she could.

'Tonight,' he said decisively, 'I'll do the pintxo tour. About 8 pm would be good.'

Relieved he had picked something off her carefully curated list, she smiled. 'I'll check availability, but I'm sure that will be fine,' she told him, feeling sorry for poor Anja having to put up with him for three hours.

'Good. And I'd like you to come too,' he added, standing up and picking up his bag, swinging it easily over his shoulder.

Disconcerted, Abi hesitated. She hadn't expected to

have to spend time with her guests beyond the odd meeting to discuss plans. Especially not with this insufferable man.

'I... I'm not sure,' she stuttered, pushing the hair that had strayed from its band out of her eyes.

'Come on, it won't be that bad,' he grinned. 'And I'm sure it will delight Adam and Peter to hear how well you are looking after me.'

Her mind was blank in her panic. 'Adam and Peter?'

'Yes,' he said, looking at her as if she was slightly deranged. 'Adam Flynn and Peter Williams of Sublime Retreats, your bosses?'

Oh God, she thought, he knows them. *Shit*. She plastered the best professional smile she could muster onto her face. 'Yes, of course. It's fine. I'll meet you downstairs at 7:30 and we can go and meet the guide.' Gathering her things together, she got ready to make her escape. 'So, if there's nothing else?'

'I will need some shopping delivered. I'll text you a list shortly,' he said dismissively, and walked out of the room with his bag.

Abigail resisted the temptation to slam the front door on her way out and stomped down the stairs and up the street, muttering under her breath all the way. Her phone chimed as she was walking back across the bridge and she looked at the unknown number, knowing exactly who it was. Yup, a shopping list. No please, no thank you. Just a list. What a jerk!

Why, oh why, does he have to be my first guest? I can't believe I am going to have to put up with him for a week, she mused angrily as she marched up to her aunt's apartment. How am I going to keep my cool around this man?

CHAPTER SEVEN

She banged into her aunt's apartment, startling the old woman who was dozing on the sofa still. May sat up, watching with interest as Abi flung her bag to the floor, then stomped into the kitchen, flinging open cupboard doors and slamming them shut again before slapping the coffee machine on.

'Someone got your coat, dear?' she called through to her niece. Momentarily stumped by her aunt's delightfully free form use of the English language, Abi paused until her brain caught up with Aunt May's. She poked her head back through the doorway, smiling despite the turmoil in her head.

'You could say that, May. You won't believe it, but my first guest is that man from the exhibition.'

May, who was still feeling a little worse for wear, took a moment to think before her face lit up. 'Oooh. Mr Unusual? How interesting,' she said, standing up and pulling the blanket around her as she shuffled into the kitchen.

'It is not interesting,' fumed Abi, 'it's bloody annoying. *He* is bloody annoying and a complete jerk!' She grabbed two cups and banged them on the counter. 'Coffee?' she demanded.

'Yes, please.' May looked at Abi with glee. 'What's so annoying about him?' she asked innocently.

'He's just... he's just. Oh, I don't know. He just is, OK? And I am stuck with him for a week!' responded Abi, as she stared at the coffee pumping out of the machine. She handed her aunt the cup. 'What are you grinning at?'

'Well,' she took a tentative sip, 'it's just unusual to see someone get under your skin like this.'

'So? What difference does that make?' Abi retorted, grabbing her cup and flouncing back through to the lounge and taking a seat at the table.

Deciding it best not to push the conversation any further, May changed tack. 'So, what do you need to organise for Mr Unusual, anyway?'

'Well, the main thing he has asked me to organise is a day where he can take the orphans out for a trip.'

May's eyebrows shot up. 'Wow, that sounds great. Those poor kids don't have much fun, that place is badly under-funded. He doesn't sound so bad,' she couldn't help but add.

'Trust me, May. He is. This might seem like an altruistic act, but I'm pretty sure there is something behind it. It's probably a tax dodge or something,' she replied snippily.

May sat quietly for a moment before piping up. 'If I could just play devil's avocado for a moment. Maybe the reason you are reacting like this is that you are attracted to him?'

Abi chuckled and glanced at her aunt. 'I can't deny that he is very attractive, May. But I am not interested. He is a pain in the arse. He is arrogant and only here for a week. And to be honest, even if I were interested in getting involved with someone right now, it absolutely would not be with Gabe Xavier,' she said with conviction.

Gabe was sitting at the table in the lounge of El Carrusel, gazing out the window at the sea. He'd unpacked his bag once he had heard Abigail leave, but images of her kept leaping into his mind. He couldn't put a finger on what it was about her, but he felt startlingly attracted to her. She was not his usual type, and he was struggling to act normally around her. He scoffed as he recalled the look of horror on her face when he had said he wanted her to come with him tonight. Flaunting the names of her bosses at her had been a low blow. Why had he done that? He never had to resort to underhanded tactics to get a woman to spend time with him, her disinterest was intriguing.

He shook his head and opened his MacBook to sort through his emails. Poor Marianna had been trying to hold down the fort, but his going AWOL for a few days never helped her cause. He had to cut free once in a while, but he didn't know why. Turn off his phone and disappear for a day or two. It gave him a sense of freedom, well, for a while. Until the guilt of responsibility crept back in. Abandoning people was his mother's forte. And Anne's.

Settling in to catch up with his work, it was only when there was a knock on the door that he lifted his head again. He stood and stretched out his cramped muscles before going to answer it. It was his groceries, as promised, and he settled the bill and gave the young delivery boy a tip which was greeted with a big smile.

Carrying the two brown paper bags through to the kitchen, he unpacked them and put everything away. He hadn't ordered much. Not in the habit of cooking for himself often, it was mostly cured meats, local cheeses, things he could snack on. He had a couple of hours until the tour, so he made up a plate, poured himself a glass of white wine and took them out to the terrace to enjoy the view. Father Thomas's words came back to him. 'Take time to enjoy yourself,' and he smiled and raised the glass in a silent toast to his friend.

Father Thomas was the only one who had been able to break through the defensive shield he had thrown up as a boy. Abandoned as a baby on the steps of the church that they had named him after, Gabe had been at the orphanage for years, occasionally going to stay with families who might adopt him but constantly being sent back, never truly knowing why. He learned not to trust anyone, apart from the priest, who was always there for him.

That is, until Anne. When he was eight, he went to stay with her, and for the first time in his young life felt like he had found a home. She was fun, but firm. She didn't put up with any of his crap, and he begrudgingly respected her for it. They settled into a routine, and he flourished under her care. He started to do better at school and become involved with extracurricular activities. He joined the debate team and the chess club, excelling at both.

But then she met a new man, Joe. He seemed OK at the start, but it soon became clear he didn't like Gabe and resented the time she spent with him. He wanted a family of his own, not this street urchin who looked at him with barely controlled anger. They got engaged and planned the wedding, and Gabe was slowly pushed out of the picture.

When she had eventually, inevitably, let him down, and he found himself back at the orphanage, it had been devastating, and he had become determined not to rely on anyone ever again. That's why he didn't do relationships, would never do relationships. He couldn't trust anyone enough to let down his guard.

Abi was looking in the mirror, applying her make-up. She looked at the eventual result and then viciously scrubbed it off again with a wipe. Why the hell was she making an effort for Mr Bloody Xavier? She settled for a flick of mascara and smoothed down her hair and went through to the lounge to get her jacket. Aunt May was out on the balcony looking through a catalogue of artist supplies and sipping on a glass of wine.

'I'm off, May,' Abi announced, bending to kiss her cheek. 'I won't be late.'

'You be as late as you like, love,' May said with a grin. 'Oh, while I remember, are you still up for joining me at the protest tomorrow?'

'For sure, that works out perfectly. I have to pop into the orphanage to complete the plans for the day out and reassure them we are not planning to kidnap the children,' she laughed.

'Well, I can understand them being a little suspicious. It's extraordinarily unusual. But then he is, isn't he?' she said wickedly with a chortle.

She slapped her aunt playfully on the shoulder. 'Behave yourself, May, and give it a rest. This is just work, and that's all it will ever be, so get those matchmaking ideas out of your head.'

'Fair enough,' she responded doubtfully. 'Either way, have a good time tonight. I'm meeting Pedro for dinner, so I might still be out when you get back.'

'Oh, yes?' Abi arched an eyebrow at her.

'What's that supposed to mean?' asked May, wrong-footed for once.

Abi looked at her for a moment before diving in. You do know that man is in love with you?

'What? I'm not... I mean, he's not,' May blustered.

'May, I've seen the way he looks at you and he most definitely is.' She told her earnestly.

'I'm sure you're wrong,' said May, but looked uncertain. 'We're good friends, yes. And we have become closer in these last years after his wife passed, but that's all it is.' She finished resolutely.

'Have it your own way,' Abi laughed, pulling her jacket on. 'Anyway, I'd better be off. I don't want to be late and give my first guest something to complain about!' She kissed her aunt again and left her sitting, gazing thoughtfully out at nothing.

Striding down the street, Abi was feeling confident that she could handle the evening ahead. She had opted for jeans and a t-shirt, comfortable and not in any way suggestive clothes. Also, she had spoken with Anya to make sure the night went smoothly, and more importantly, swiftly. She arrived at the street door two minutes early and found him waiting for her.

'Good evening, Mr Xavier' she said cheerfully, her eyes taking in the snug-fitting jeans and blue t-shirt combo he was wearing. He looked her up and down and smiled.

'Looks like we've opted for the same outfit.' He chuckled, 'and please call me Gabe. It feels like I'm at work when you call me Mr Xavier.'

Laughing despite herself, 'OK, Gabe it is. Shall we?' she gestured along the street and they began to walk, falling into step as she told him some of the history of San Sebastian. Well, what she had memorised so far. It didn't take long for them to arrive at the first bar where they were meeting Anya, and she realised he had been amiable company. *This is going to be a doddle,* she thought, greeting Anya with a kiss and making the introductions.

Anya had secured a small table in the corner of the bar, which was becoming busier by the minute. Abi found herself squeezed in next to Gabe on the bench against the wall. With his thigh touching hers and heat radiating from his body, she gulped. She was hyper-aware of the contact, her body supersensitive to every pressure where their limbs met. Maybe not such a doddle after all. Trying to edge imperceptibly away as Anya went to get the first of the wines they would taste, she could see from the corner of her eye that Gabe was looking around with interest, apparently unaware of her.

When Anya returned, Abi grabbed her glass and took a hefty slug of the white wine before registering Anya's look of disapproval.

'This,' the young woman announced pointedly, 'is the first of many local wines you will be tasting tonight. It is a chardonnay from the San Sebastian Winery and it has won many awards.'

She gestured for them to take a sip as a waiter brought over some pintxos. Gabe took a moment to smell the wine before taking a sip. He'd obviously done this before. Abi's stomach growled, and she realised she hadn't eaten since breakfast and dived into the delicious-looking plates of food. Taking a huge bite from the bread laden with anchovies and green peppers, she had to grab a napkin to catch some of the toppings which slid down her chin.

Looking to her right, she saw Gabe watching her with amusement. 'What?' she demanded.

'Nothing, it's just nice to see a woman enjoying her food, is all.' He looked genuine, but she took a daintier bite this time and tried to keep most of it in her mouth. The next round of wine arrived, and they continued to taste and try the various pintxos that appeared like magic every time a plate emptied.
Abi was really enjoying herself and it seemed that Gabe was, too. He was chatting away with Anya, asking questions and tasting everything with enthusiasm.

The fact that they had somehow gotten closer on the bench, the full length of his body touching hers, occasionally leaning in further as he included her in something he was saying, was playing havoc with Abi's libido. When he stood to follow Anya to the next bar, the sudden cold came as a shock. He looked down at her.

'Are you coming?' he smiled.

Her brain was in naughty schoolgirl mode, and she had to bite back the retort that was springing to her lips. *I'd better slow down on the wine*, she admonished herself as they walked up the bustling street. She needed to keep her runaway mouth in check.

Night time was a social time in San Sebastian. Families, couples and students alike were roaming the streets. Popping in and out of bars, the sound of greetings and laughter filled the air. It was invigorating. She loved the sense of community here, so very different from her home in London.

The second bar was more modern than the first, the pintxos a little more gourmet but equally tasty. Abi made a point of only taking a sip of each wine and drinking some water in between this time. Sat across the table from Gabe, she felt a little more in control and relaxed a bit. She watched him as he chatted comfortably with Anya. He undoubtedly was quite gorgeous; she could be tempted in other circumstances. It's a shame he's such an arse.

But she wasn't here to find a man. She was here to take back control of her life that had slipped so effortlessly off its rails in the last six months. And her priority was to be successful in her new job. That was what she needed to focus on and she couldn't let tall, handsome, irritating strangers distract from her mission.

CHAPTER EIGHT

The last port of call for the evening was Baztan Pintxos & Bar, where Miquel's face lit up when he saw Abi through the usual crowd at the bar. 'Abi!' he called out over the noisy throng. 'How are you?' he asked as he pushed his way through to give her an extended hug.

'I'm good, Miquel,' she replied, extracting herself. 'This is Gabe,' she turned to the side so he could see the man standing behind her. His face dropped for a moment as he took in the handsome man standing there, but then rallied, a smile reappearing on his face like a mask.

'Welcome, welcome. Any friend of Abi's is a friend of ours,' he said congenially, keeping his plastic smile in place. Anya stepped forward and punched her brother on the arm.

'This is the first guest staying at the apartment that Abi is the concierge at you fool. I booked a table for us, remember?'

Miquel's face was a picture, but it lit up again, with relief this time.

'Oh, yes. Of course. Please follow me,' and he led them around the bar to the table with a plaque on it announcing, 'Erreserbatuta.'

'Here you are,' he smiled at them. 'Get yourselves seated and I will bring the first bottle of wine you are tasting here tonight.'

Watching the young man make his way back behind the bar with hooded eyes, Gabe waited for the girls to be seated before sliding in next to Abi.

'Looks like someone has a bit of a crush on you.' He turned to look at her, his eyes dark and unreadable as they bored into hers.

'What? Miquel? No, no, we're just friends,' Abi said, averting her eyes from the intensity of his gaze.

'I would disagree,' he growled, then was quiet for a moment. 'So, Anya,' he said eventually, laser focusing his attention on the girl. 'Tell me a little about yourself.' The young woman melted under his appraising look and flushed prettily, adding an extra glow to her sun-kissed skin.

'There's not much to tell you, Gabe,' she replied, suddenly shy. 'Born and raised in San Sebastian, I will doubtless live here forever,' she giggled as Miquel returned with a tray bearing the next round of wine and food.

'Please, let me,' said Gabe. He reached across to take

the bottle and poured her a glass of wine before filling his own, then placed it back on the table.

'So, what do I need to know about this one?' he asked, sloshing it deftly around the glass while keeping his gaze on the young girl sitting across from him.

As the guide began her tale of where and how the wine was made, Abi sat there fuming. She picked up the bottle and poured herself a healthy measure before banging it back on the table and sullenly sat there drinking. He was flirting with Anya, no doubt about that, she thought between irate gulps. Not that she cared!

By the time she had finished her glass and the next bottle had arrived, she was feeling like the third wheel at the table and was getting angrier by the moment. *I will not react; I will not react,* she muttered to herself like a mantra, trying to curb her resentment as the other two continued to talk animatedly, completely ignoring her.

When he repeated the process, serving the wine only for the two of them a second time, she stood up abruptly, unable to contain it any longer. Looking down at their surprised faces, she tried to keep her voice even as she said, 'Sorry, guys. I'm not feeling too well. I hope you don't mind if I leave you in Anya's capable hands, Gabe?' she added, glaring at him.

She didn't wait for a reply and forced her way through the crowd in front of the bar, pushing her way outside. The cooler evening air of the cobbled street was a relief. What a jerk! She stomped up the street. I mean, of course, he is free to flirt with whoever he damn chooses, but he doesn't have to be so rude. She marched home, her anger dissipating a little with each step. By the time she reached the front door, she was feeling guilty for leaving like that. What if he complained to Sublime Retreats? What if they decided she wasn't a good concierge and wanted someone else for the job?

Damn her fiery nature. She blamed it on the red hair. She never could keep her cool, could never keep her mouth shut when she should. It always got her into trouble. Making her way slowly up the stairs, she could hear her aunt singing away and as she opened the door to the apartment, she found her dancing around the lounge with a broom in her arms and Bob joyfully squawking along on her shoulder. She stood, watching her for a moment, a quizzical smile on her face, entranced by the image.

'Did you have a good evening, May?' she called. May dropped the broom in surprise and whirled around, her face alight with happiness.

'I did,' the woman beamed at her. 'I most certainly did,' she confirmed, placing a disgruntled Bob on the driftwood perch she had created for him in the corner of the room.

Walking in and placing her bag on the whitewashed dining table, she cocked a knowing eyebrow at her. 'Pedro?'

'Yes, Pedro,' repeated May girlishly, sinking onto the sofa and patting the cushion next to her. Forgetting her anger for a moment, Abi went and sat on the sofa and looked expectantly at her.

'You were right, it seems, my dear,' May's face was glowing. 'What you said about Pedro was playing on my mind all night and in the end, I had to ask him.'

'I can see from your face you got a positive response,' laughed Abi. 'But wasn't that a bit risky? If I had been wrong, it would have been exceedingly awkward, especially as you work together.'

May took hold of both her hands and gazed at her. 'Abi, sometimes you have to take a leap of faith and see where it leads you,' she said, looking serious for a moment before the brilliant smile returned. 'If I had said nothing, how many more years would we have wasted before that silly man got up the courage to say something?'

Abi laughed, and hearing her phone chirping, stood and went to retrieve it from her bag. Seeing it was a message from Gabe, she muttered 'talking of silly men,' and clicked to read it.

'What time are we going to the protest tomorrow, May?'

'In the morning, sweetheart. Why?'

'Mr Unusual wants to do the coastal tour tomorrow. I'll tell him we can do it in the afternoon,' she said, rapidly tapping out her response.

'So, how did it go this evening?' May asked curiously, watching Abi's face. She chucked her phone back onto the table before replying. 'So, so. I mean, he seemed to enjoy what San Sebastian offers,' she added churlishly, pushing her hair out of her eyes.

Intrigued, May stood up and walked to the kitchen. 'I'll just get us a glass of wine, then you can tell me all about it,' she called back over her shoulder.

Sitting on the balcony, sipping her wine and watching the moon reflecting off the sea in the distance, Abi felt a lot calmer, having got everything off her chest.

'Well, it sounds to me like you may have reacted a bit... Well, a bit quickly,' May said after she had described the evening to her. 'Sure, it was rude of him not to serve your wine, but he's completely within his rights to flirt with Anya. Especially as you have no interest in him,' she grinned at her.

'Yes, I know,' Abi replied, sinking back into her seat. 'His message just now was friendly enough, so hopefully he hasn't taken any offence at me leaving so suddenly. I don't want him complaining to Peter and Adam about me.'

'You can make it up to him tomorrow on the coastal tour. Be extra attentive, show him the fun Abi, just to be sure.'

'Humph,' came the reply. 'We'll see. I'll do my best, but he's so annoying it's going to be difficult.'

Gabe was sitting on the terrace back at his apartment, looking at the same reflections of the big silver moon and wondering what it was about Abigail Johnson that made him behave like such an idiot. What had possessed him to exclude her like that in that last bar? He knew she was pissed with him. Despite what she had said about not feeling well, he recognised an angry woman when he saw one. Let's face it, he'd seen enough of them.

He had felt bad as soon as she marched out of the place but, obligated to finish up the wine tasting tour, he had obediently sat and listened to the young woman extolling the virtues of the remaining wines before making his escape. His mind had reeled, twisting and turning on the walk back to the apartment and as he had paused in front of the carousel. There was something about her that couldn't be ignored, and he was not used to losing control of his feelings like this. The fact was, he worked damn hard to make sure it didn't happen. He was famous for his steely resolve.

Relieved when she had responded to his message about the tour tomorrow so swiftly, he smiled and put his phone on the table. Not that he had any interest in being ferried up and down the coast to look at old buildings, but it was all that he could think of at short notice that gave him an excuse to spend some more time with her. And he wanted to spend more time with her. It was against everything he held dear as far as women were concerned, but he wanted to get to know her, see what made her tick. If he could work out what made her so different, then maybe he could put up a defence against it and get on with his life.

Sighing, he picked up his phone again and called Father Thomas on a whim.

'Gabe, my boy,' came the cheery reply. 'How the devil are you?'

'I'm good, Father. Just thought I'd check in and see how the new roof is coming along?'

Father Thomas gave a barking laugh, which turned into a protracted cough that took a moment to pass.

'Are you OK?' Gabe asked with concern.

'I'm fine, nothing to worry about, just a bit of a cold,' said the priest breezily. 'I was laughing because you generally only call me when you are feeling out of sorts. Has something over there upset you?'

He smiled into the handset. The old man was no fool, that was for sure. 'Absolutely not,' he said resolutely, ignoring the image of Abigail laughing, her hazel eyes sparkling, that rose to taunt him. 'As I said, I wanted to check on how the work is going. I do have a vested interest, you know.'

'Fair enough,' Thomas replied. 'It's going exceptionally well. The building firm you recommended is going great guns. I think they may well finish it ahead of schedule.'

Pleased that the guys were following his instructions, Gabe felt a little more in control. 'That's great news. And by the way, I'll be going to the orphanage the day after tomorrow. I can have a look at what's going on there and move forward with that idea I told you about.'

'That's wonderful news, son. I didn't doubt that you would forge ahead to make the most of this opportunity. You are taking some time out, though, aren't you?'

'Yes, Father, I am. In fact, tomorrow I am going on a tour of the region, exploring the coastline. Is that relaxing enough for you?'

The priest coughed again, long, drawn-out rasps, and concern wrinkled Gabe's brow.

'You have been to see the doctor, haven't you?'

'It's just a piddling little cold, Gabe. Nothing to worry about. It's those pesky kids, you know what bug fests they are at this time of year. Don't fret.'

Not reassured, and frustrated that he was so far away, Gabe made a note to call the priest again tomorrow after the tour. The notion that the old man might be seriously ill flashed like ice through his body and his head throbbed faintly.

'Anyway. I have to run,' Father Thomas was saying. 'Keep me posted about the project and do try to have a good time while you're there.'

Saying his goodbyes, Gabe sat for a while, looking at the view and worrying about Father Thomas. He could see the lights of the carousel spinning below him and he heard the shrieks of the children enjoying the ride. He was at a bit of a loss for what to do; not feeling tired right now. His body clock was all out of whack and insisting that it was daytime. It was unusual for him to have free time to fill. Every minute of every day was ordinarily accounted for with meetings, or planning, or schmoozing the next deal.

What did people normally do? He went inside and turned on the TV, idly flicking through the channels. Maybe he could find something there to distract himself.

CHAPTER NINE

Abi woke up early the next morning but lay in bed for a while, pondering her life. She was enjoying being here with Aunt May, but it felt more like a holiday instead of a life-changing decision. She couldn't see where she slotted in here in Spain, didn't feel quite at home. The job with Sublime Retreats was ideal for now. Or rather, once she got rid of Gabe Xavier it would be.

She was emailing with the groups coming in the following weeks, who were all very keen to do everything she suggested, and she felt confident that they would have a fantastic time. They seemed like normal holidaymakers looking to make the most of their time.

In the meantime, what to do with Gabe? His brooding eyes floated into view, that knowing spark deep within them hinting that he understood her. Truly saw her and perceived what her treacherous brain was thinking about. It was so disconcerting and made her tummy lurch in such a peculiar way. She didn't know how to cope with it.

Hearing sounds of activity coming from the kitchen, she pulled herself out of bed and went to the bathroom before joining her aunt for what had become their morning ritual of coffee on the balcony.

'Good morning, Sunshine,' May greeted her as Bob flew past, spitefully pecking her cheek before flying off over the rooftops for his morning exercise. Abi stopped in her tracks, rubbing her bruised face and glowered at her.

'Don't call me that,' she bleated, plonking herself on the balcony chair, furiously pulling at the cotton robe that had rucked up awkwardly under her.

'Someone woke up on the wrong side of their head,' her aunt continued gaily, but even this failed to raise a smile. 'What's up with you?'

'Sorry, May. It's just that's what Dad used to call me.' Abi said, taking her first sip of coffee with relish, closing her eyes and leaning her head back a little to absorb more sun on her face.

May sat remarkably quiet for a few minutes. 'Have you spoken to him recently?' she asked speculatively, looking at her niece's face for a reaction.

'No, I have not. I have no intention of doing so either.' She replied without hesitation, eyes snapping open as she sat up straight.

'Lily would be sad that you still weren't speaking to him, you know?'

Looking sharply at May, she banged her cup down. 'That's a low blow! How dare you bring mum into this?' she huffed at her morning hair that was falling across her face in messy fronds.

'I dare to bring her into it because she was my sister.' May said firmly. 'And it would break her heart to see you still estranged from him.'

'He decided to bugger off and leave us. He chose to have another life. I am not to blame here.'

'I know that, sweetheart. We all know that. But he and your mum weren't happy. You must remember the arguments?'

She did. Those huge, never-ending, vicious rows that had her hiding in the garden. The blissful peace when he left almost made up for his absence. Then mum got her diagnosis and her world turned upside down yet again.

'Yeah, but then she got ill. He should have come back then,' she said stubbornly, looking up in surprise when May chuckled, the sound so out of place in this conversation.

'The last thing poor Lily needed was him being there when she was coping with her chemo and her guilt at leaving you to fend for yourself.'

Tears sprang to Abi's eyes. She rubbed them furiously with the back of her hands, before asking softly, 'she felt guilty?'

'Yes! Of course she did. You were scarcely fifteen,

and she knew she was going to die no matter how hard she fought. She begged me to take you back to Spain with me, but you insisted on staying to finish school, remember?'

Abi had tried to forget that dreadful time in her life, but she did remember her insistence on finishing off school. Although she realised now it had been more to do with the fear of the unknown. She had lost her dad and was losing her mum. She had needed something familiar to remain the same. With a start, she looked at May.

'I don't think I ever thanked you for spending that time with me.'

'Oh pish, no need for that.'

'You left your life for a year to support me,' she insisted, only now understanding what a huge, selfless thing that had been. Her teenage-self had been oblivious to the sacrifice May had made for her.

Her aunt smiled her sunny smile. 'It was my pleasure, Abi. But one of the last things Lily asked of me, apart from taking care of you, was to help mend the fences between you and your dad.'

Abi scowled into her coffee cup, looking exactly as she had as a teenager.

'He offered to come back, you know?'

'What?'

'He came to see Lily in the hospital that first round,

and offered to come back, but she shot him down in flames. Your mum knew it was pointless, and to be honest, she was happier without him.'

'I... I didn't realise.'

'Lily didn't want you to know. I think she was afraid you would end up hating her as much as you think you hate him.'

Abi sat back, stunned. She had spent all this time believing he had cheerfully abandoned them and ignored them in their hour of need. She remembered of all the times he had tried to reach out to her, all the times she had laughed bitterly in his face and he hadn't said a word. A lump formed in her throat.

'So, please, for your mum, consider at least talking to him? You were always so close when you were little.'

She nodded slowly in response, her mind reeling at these revelations.

'Anyway,' May said brightly. 'Enough of this talk. Let's go save a nature reserve, shall we?'

Relief flooded through her, the prospect of taking action a welcome distraction, and Abi jumped up. 'I'll just have a quick wash and get dressed.' She ducked as a flash of brilliant red and electric blue alerted her a second before Bob came sailing back through the doorway, cackling noisily. *That bird is a demon*, she thought as she tightly closed her bathroom door. She had discovered yesterday that if you didn't, he liked to join you in the shower and that had not been a fun experience.

The old camper van spluttered and coughed into life and they drove out of town towards the protest in companionable silence. When they arrived, they could see things were a little more frenzied than usual. There were more protesters for a start, and they were running around like a disturbed ant's nest.

'What's going on?' called May to the first person she could catch.

'We've heard from a reliable source that there is a property developer here, looking to buy the land!' the young girl said urgently as she flew past.

'Well, we can't be having that. Come on, Abi,' her aunt responded, marching determinedly towards the dominant group where there was a hubbub of raised voices as everyone tried to get their point across. May stood, listening for a moment, then nodded before calling out, 'Abi can do it.' Her voice was loud enough to make them all stop, and turn to her in surprise, Abi included.

'What? What can I do?' Abi asked, sotto voiced, panic-stricken at what her aunt was volunteering her for.

'Abi here did a great job in organising the promotion of my art exhibition. I'm sure she will do an equally fabulous job of getting the media involved and raising awareness for us. Let the people know what's going on here.'

All eyes focused on her, and the familiar warmth crept up her neck. Damn her complexion.

'Is that true?' called out an older man, leaning on his placard, the end sinking into the grass. 'Will you be able to get the attention we require to stop this dreadful plan?'

'I can certainly give it my best shot,' said Abi, sounding braver than she felt. 'What we need is a few of us to work on this. Has anyone here had any experience in marketing?'

A few cautious hands raised in the crowd. 'OK, you three, come with me and we'll start planning our assault. The rest of you carry on. Create as much noise as you can!'

On the drive back to town, Abi's head was buzzing with ideas, caught up in the cause and determined to make a difference. It was only as they pulled into the parking space and she realised the time that she remembered she had to meet Gabe. Glancing down at her scruffy, mud-splattered jeans and pulling at the ancient t-shirt she had put on in haste this morning, she cursed. It would have to do. She didn't have time to go back to the apartment and change. She found him standing by the carousel, watching its endless rounds as if mesmerised.

'Good morning, Gabe,' she called to get his attention, and he spun around, his eyes roaming her body in a leisurely fashion before he met her gaze. *God*, Abi thought, *what must he think of me*?

'Sorry about this,' she waved her hand to take in her outfit, then self-consciously patted down her hair. 'I was doing something this morning and didn't have time to change.'

Smirking, he drawled, 'not a problem. Shabby chic is in right now, apparently.'

Her hackles rose in response. It seemed to be a regular occurrence around this man. Gabe, of course, was looking dashing. Casually dressed but with discreet labels, letting her know his outfit doubtless cost more than her entire wardrobe. Abi tried to keep the smile on her face as she said, 'anyway, come this way. I've arranged for us to meet the car over there.' She pointed over to the parking area, and they fell into step as they walked towards it.

Their driver and guide for the day was a lovely man called Anton. He looked to be somewhere in his fifties and his expressive brown eyes shone with excitement as he climbed out of the black sedan to meet them.

'Welcome, welcome. I will be driving you today, and what a wonderful day it is going to be,' he said happily as he opened the rear door for them before sliding back into the driver's seat. As he started the engine, he continued. 'Our first stop is going to be the marvellous cathedral at Bayonne. Have either of you heard of it?'

They both shook their heads, and Abi tried to concentrate as Anton gushed forth, a mine of information. But Gabe's proximity was playing havoc with her senses. He was shower-fresh, she noticed with her furtive glances, his blonde hair still curling damply at the nape of his neck, and she could smell his cologne. She squirmed in her seat, and here she was looking like something the cat had dragged in.

'Everything OK?' Gabe turned to her, that knowing twinkle dancing annoyingly in his blue eyes.

'Completely fine,' she snapped. 'Now concentrate on what Anton is telling us.'

'Yes, ma'am,' he chuckled, but duly returned his gaze to the front and Anton.

Gabe's attention was anywhere but with the guide. Abi looked so damn gorgeous. He was having a hard time not reaching over and messing up that wonderful red hair even further. Straining to make sense of what Anton was telling them, he asked a couple of pertinent questions, a trick he'd learned in school, to give the appearance of being focused.

Thankfully, Anton was an excellent guide, and as he drove the car smoothly out of the city and onto the open road, he chatted comfortably about the history of the region and they both found themselves being drawn in. Signs for Bayonne appeared, flashing by at the side of the road, and soon they were driving across the river Adour into the city.

Once Anton had found somewhere to park, they walked through the narrow medieval streets into the heart of the city, where the cathedral's two spires dominated. The guide led them through the doors to the main chapel and, in hushed tones, explained the history of the gothic building. Abi found her feet taking her forward, impossibly attracted to the stained-glass windows above the pulpit. She stood there in a trance, looking up, admiring their beauty and the colours.

'It looks like something your aunt would paint,' declared Gabe right next to her, startling her out of her reverie. She glanced at him. He was standing, chin tilted up, gazing at the windows in awe. Even in this dim light, she could detect the gleam in his brooding eyes.

'You're right,' she said, turning her gaze back to the windows. 'She would love the colours. I wonder if she has been here.'

Anton touched her arm, to show they should move on, and they went out to the cloisters, where the fantastic stonework of the arcade had Gabe astonished.

'I've never seen work like this,' he announced passionately, running his hand admiringly down the fretted stone columns. Abi smiled at his boyish enthusiasm as they wandered along the worn flagstones and she imagined the hundreds of years of passage and feet that had pitted yet polished them as time passed.

'So, are you in the building industry?' she asked,

realising she had no clue about his profession. He paused, looking at her. 'Something like that, yes,' he replied, a shutter coming down, his face returning to its previous passive, slightly sneering demeanour. Feeling like she'd been shut out suddenly, Abi called to Anton. 'I guess it's time we left,' and the guide capered over, visibly excited about the next port of call.

'We are going to head to the coast later, but first I want to show you something, Abi. Everyone loves Chocolate Street.' He was right, she did. The short street was a smorgasbord of delight for any chocolate lover, which she undeniably was. Gabe seemed as delighted as she was, the previous chill dissipating as he tried sample after sample with her. Some of the chocolatiers had been there for over a hundred years and the insane amount of choice had her head spinning.

They walked from shop to shop, trying everything on offer with enthusiasm, laughing at each other's excitement at discovery.

'You have to try this, Gabe,' she called to him. 'It's sensational.' She proffered a spoon in his direction.
'Does your role as concierge include spoon-feeding me too?' he asked as he walked towards her, taking in her beautiful hazel eyes, wide with excitement, and her usually pale cheeks lightly flushed. There was a smudge of chocolate on her chin. She looked adorable, and he felt a heat rising in his body that would not be suppressed.

Giggling, she spooned a mouthful of dark chocolate

mousse into his waiting mouth. Looking at his lips, parted to try this latest discovery, she couldn't help but lick her own. His eyes caught the movement, and widened, the pupils dilating as they locked back onto hers.

'You should try the chocolate bonbons; the ginger, the pistache, or the espelette pepper ones,' the assistant was saying, but neither of them responded. Gabe felt suspended in the moment. The air glittering between them, and the rising heat in his body would be forever interwoven in his mind with the explosion of the taste of mousse melting in his mouth.

They both took a step back, a little breathless, not sure what had just happened. Abi looked around furtively. Surely everyone could sense the spark that had just flown between them? Gabe stood up straight and called to the guide that he wanted to leave in a tone that had Anton looking surprised, but he bobbed his head in acquiescence and they walked back to the car.

The short drive down the coast to the next location of the tour was largely silent. Anton, picking up that something was amiss with these two but not knowing what, kept his commentary brief but to the point. He pulled the car in and twisted around to consider at them thoughtfully.

'Here's your chance to walk off some of that chocolate before we go for lunch,' he pointed across to a metal walkway leading out to sea. A bizarre rock formation with a statue balanced precariously on it could be seen at the end.

'Aren't you coming with us?' Abi asked hopefully. She didn't want to be alone with Gabe. Not now, not ever.

'No, these old legs have seen ol' Mary over there enough times. You young ones go over, get your photos for Instagram or whatnot and I'll meet you back here in a bit.' He pulled a newspaper out of the glove compartment and rustled it open, brooking no argument.

Gabe climbed out, holding the door for Abi, neither of them daring to look at the other as they made their way to the flimsy-looking bridge. Going across in silence, the crowds of returning tourists forced them closer together, arms bumping occasionally. The wind had picked up and, surrounded by the crashing waves that highlighted the dramatic rocks, the tension between them eased as they took in the beauty of their surroundings. They walked through the tunnel carved out of the rock that the Virgin Mary balanced upon and stood on the viewing point on the other side, looking out to sea.

'I guess we should take some pictures,' Abi said finally, pulling out her phone and snapping at the glorious view.

'Haven't you been here before?' Gabe asked, following suit and taking a few shots of his own.

'Er, no. I've not been here in Spain long,' Abi said

cautiously, unsure whether as a concierge for Sublime Retreats she should admit to that.

'Well, you seem pretty clued up on the place for a newbie,' he replied. 'Do you realise Anton is sick of us already?' he grinned at her. She laughed.
'He did seem in a hurry to get rid of us.'

'Shall we go and annoy him some more?' he enquired with a cheeky grin, proffering his arm, his bicep rippling and already showing signs of a tan.

'Let's do that,' she gulped, threading her arm through his with a smile, and they made their way back across the causeway. His skin was soft and smooth over his hard muscles, she couldn't help but notice as she tried to concentrate on what he was saying, but it wasn't easy.

Looking at the young couple returning, smiling and chatting freely arm in arm, Anton grinned at his reflection in the rear-view mirror. Nobody could visit Rocher de la Vierge and stay mad with one another for long.

CHAPTER TEN

Thirty minutes later, they were pulling into the lovely town of Port de Saint-Jean-de-Luz, with its jumble of whitewashed buildings topped with rust-coloured tiles, clustered around the harbour, and as Anton drove along the seafront, several people walking down the street and sitting in the cafes hailed him.

'Seems like they know you pretty well here,' Gabe said, looking about with interest.

'They should. I was born here,' the guide replied, glancing back at him proudly, slowing the car as a dog ran into the road. They all looked on in horror as it stopped dead centre and squatted, unashamedly, to do its business. An embarrassed silence filled the car as they all watched, unable to drag their eyes away from the scene until the dog finished with a quick, satisfied kick of its back legs and then trotted gaily off.

'This used to be the centre of the fishing industry locally, even whaling in the past.' Anton continued bravely, as if nothing had happened, and the car moved forward again. 'Now we make do with sardines and tuna, the best you will find in Spain!'

Abi grinned at Gabe. She was getting hungry. 'That sounds promising,' she said happily. 'Is there somewhere you would recommend for lunch?'

'Well, you can, of course, go anywhere you like. There are many wonderful places here. But if I can suggest that place over there?' He pointed at a restaurant across the street, just as a young man walked out, and seeing Anton, waved vigorously. 'That is my cousin, Ager. He and his family have run the place for many, many years and their food is second to none.'

'Seems rude not to,' muttered Gabe with a smile to Abi. She nodded, and they climbed out and hurried over the road between the passing traffic. The restaurant inside was small and quite dark, the walls cheesily covered with all the trappings of fishing and life at sea. But the smells coming from the kitchen were exquisite, so they sat down eagerly and studied the menu.

'Welcome, my friends, welcome,' cried Ager, bustling over with a carafe of Txakoli. 'Please accept this from me,' he announced, pouring the wine before they could either object or concur. 'So,' he placed the carafe on the table when he had finished, 'let me tell you about today's specials.'

He continued to reel off a list of delectable sounding dishes. Understanding the choices slightly overwhelmed them, Anton said, 'thank you, Ager, can you give us a few minutes to decide?' His cousin bowed and trotted off to the next table to clear away their empty plates.

'It all sounds so good,' said Abi, staring hopelessly up at the chalkboard with the specials listed on it.

'Well, I'm going to stick with the traditional grilled sardines,' declared Gabe decisively, closing his menu with a snap and placing it on the red and white chequered tablecloth.

'A good choice,' agreed Anton. 'I think I will have the same.' They both turned and looked at Abi, who was still dithering. 'I guess it will have to be... the Bacalao al pil-pil', she said, carefully sounding out the un-familiar words.

'Perfect,' said Anton. 'And can I suggest just a trad-itional salad on the side? It is very garlicky, but it com-plements our dishes perfectly!'

Happy to go with his choice, they settled into an easy conversation about the sights they'd seen today until Ager returned to take their orders. He wrote them down on a tiny notepad, nodding in approval at each choice.

'I will bring you some Piperrada and some bread while you wait. The Bacalao takes a little time to pre-pare,' he beamed before trotting back to the kitchen.

'So, what brings you to San Sebastian, Gabe?' Anton enquired once his cousin had left. 'Apart from the ob-vious,' he chuckled.

'Well, boss. I just needed a break, you know? And this place popped up in my inbox and looked pretty sweet, so I figured, why not?'

Startled by his sudden turn of phrase, Abi glanced at him, but he was refusing to look at her.

'So, how 'bout you? How d'ya get into the guiding business?' he asked, setting Anton off again.

As the guide's life history unravelled around them, Abi sat back, intrigued, watching Gabe. He seemed to be covering something up. She must remember to Google him when she had a moment to herself.

The meal was amazing. Anton had been right about the food here. Her cod in a creamy sauce was to die for, and judging by the way Gabe was clearing his plate, the sardines were pretty good too. They refused dessert but accepted a chilled glass of Patxaran, the sweet, reddish-brown liqueur a perfect digestive.

On the return journey to San Sebastian, Abi was leaning back in the seat, struggling to keep her eyes open. It had been a long day, and she was looking forward to getting home and having a shower.

Anton dropped them off by the carousel, Gabe discreetly passing a fold of notes to the man as they shook hands. Anton beamed at him. 'Anything you need while you are here, Gabe, just let me know,' he said and gave him a business card. They strolled towards the entrance to the apartment, discussing the plans for the rest of the week.

'You don't have anything booked for tomorrow,' Abi said, as they reached the doorway and he fished the keys out of his pocket. 'Do you want me to organise something?'

He looked thoughtful for a moment before replying. 'No, it's OK. I have some work to catch up on and I might just go for a wander about town, you know, soak up some of the atmosphere. Tuesday we're taking the kids out, right?'

'Yes, it's all arranged. I will meet the minibus, go to the orphanage, and then we can meet you back here.' She pointed to where they had just been dropped off.

Gabe shook his head. 'No. I would prefer to go with you to pick the children up.' Abi looked up at him, surprised. 'Are you sure? That means a thirty-minute drive each way, plus however long they take to get organised. Do you honestly want to sit through all that?'

'Yes, I do. I want to look at where they live,' he stated firmly, unable to meet her eyes for a moment. Then he peered down, a warm smile spreading across his face and his dimple appearing, causing an even warmer sensation to spread across her body. 'Well,' he declared, 'this is a bit odd. Usually, when I take a girl out, I walk her home, not the other way round.'

Still basking in the glow of his smile, it took a second for his words to register. When they did, she stepped back, uncertain of where they were leading. Determined to be professional, she quickly said, 'OK, well, I will meet you here on Tuesday, 9.30 sharp?' His eyes were laughing at her again. She could detect a smirk trying to edge its way onto his face, the dimple giving the game away. God, he was infuriating.

'Sure thing, Abigail,' he answered easily, raising his hand in mock salute. 'I'll see ya soon.' With that, he turned and made his way up the stairs. She watched as his feet disappeared up the stairwell. A Gabe free day tomorrow sounded like a good idea. It was going to be a relief and give her a chance to cool down a bit. Her body didn't seem to be on board with the whole 'don't let Gabe get to you' thing.

May had been out when she had got home yesterday, and judging by the singing that was coming from the kitchen this morning, she'd been with Pedro. Abi got up and found her aunt wafting around the kitchen with a dreamy smile on her face.

'I take it things are going well with Pedro?' she asked with a smile as she got herself a coffee, holding the cup in two hands, blowing on its contents impatiently before taking a sip.

'Oh, Abi. He is wonderful,' her aunt replied. 'He's so romantic. Who would have believed it at my age? We had dinner, then took a moonlit walk along the beach. And then he walked me home like a true gentleman,' she finished. That reminded Abi of Gabe's jest yesterday, and her stomach lurched. It had felt a bit like the end of a date. *And you wouldn't have minded if he had kissed you*, her inner voice taunted.

'How was your tour?' May asked, breaking into her thoughts and gesturing that they move out to the balcony. Abi grabbed a croissant off a plate on the side and followed her out into the bright, sunlit morning.

'It was fantastic,' she enthused. 'Have you been to the cathedral at Bayonne? The stained-glass windows are amazing. They would make a great subject for your painting,'

May mused for a moment. 'I have been, I'm sure. It was a long time ago though, maybe I should revisit. But my question was more to do with Mr Unusual than the tour itself,' she laughed, glancing at Abi before turning back to watch Bob as he swooped in joyful arcs in the distance, his brilliant-coloured wings glinting in the sun. Abi busied herself with the croissant, taking a large bite to give her time to consider her answer.

'Well, he's still annoying,' she said finally. 'But I think I've got a handle on him now,' she added, sounding far more certain than she felt. Did she have a handle on him? Did she have any idea how she was going to cope with being around him for the rest of the week? *That will be a big, fat no!* Her inner voice cackled gleefully.

As hard as she tried to keep the images of him out of her mind, the more they seemed to pop up. She had woken with a start from a dream where he'd been kissing her by the carousel, which was spinning in sync with the whirl of emotion and sensations that he was creating with his lips. It was most disconcerting. At least she had a free day today to shake off the effects of Gabe Xavier.

Remembering that she was going to Google him, Abi picked up her phone. Seeing there was an email from Adam Flynn, she read through it quickly, her heart sinking, as she feared it was a reprimand of some sort. But he was just checking how her first guest was getting on, so she quickly typed out a response, letting him know it was going well. *I hope to God Gabe will corroborate this,* she thought as self-doubt swirled around her mind.

A message popped up from Anya as she watched the email send, inviting her to go to the beach with Miquel and some of their friends today. Abi considered it for a moment. It was tempting. She hadn't had time to enjoy the beach yet, and she'd been here nearly a month. In truth, she hadn't had the chance to do anything much since she'd been so busy these last few weeks. What with the exhibition, the protest and getting ready to greet her first guest.

She had a free day today and if it was a group, it should still keep Miquel firmly in the friend zone and not give him any further ideas. She agreed to meet them in an hour down at La Concha and happily finished her croissant, looking forward to the day ahead.

'Don't forget to smother yourself in sun cream,' May said as Abi rose to get ready. 'With your fair skin, a day by the sea could be fatal!'

'I won't forget,' she replied. 'I'll have lashings of the stuff on, plus a hat. Don't worry, May, I'll be careful.' She hummed a jaunty tune as she got her bikini on, carefully cutting the labels off it. Another gift May had foisted upon her. She smiled. What would she do without her aunt? Collecting all the essentials and slipping them into a beach bag, she called her good-byes and set off down the street to meet her friends.

Abi returned the cheery greetings from people she passed on her journey, their faces becoming familiar now, and made good time to the beach. She glanced across to the carousel and the apartment behind it, wondering what Gabe was up to. There was a pang of guilt. Maybe she should have insisted he did some-thing today? Would Sublime Retreats frown on her taking a day off? Gnawing at her bottom lip, she stood indecisively, staring at the apartment for a moment. She fished her phone out of her bag to send him a message.

Good morning. I just wanted to check if there is anything you want me to organise today? Please let me know if you need anything.

Feeling better, she tucked the phone back in the bag and scanned the beach to find her friends.

Gabe had been awake since before dawn. He was

125

blaming it on jetlag, but knew it was in no small part because of thoughts of Abigail. That moment, yesterday, when she had fed him the chocolate mousse, had been one of the most erotic things he had encountered in his life, yet there was no reason for it.

She was just his concierge, and they had been standing in a shop, goofing around. Nothing remotely sexy about that, was there? But it had been. He couldn't deny it if he wanted to, and he didn't understand it.

As if she'd heard him, a message popped up on his phone. Let me know if you need anything. Ha! Parts of him certainly needed something, but he was going to have to try to put her out of his mind and focus on the job at hand. He checked the time; it was still early back home, but he opened his laptop and started sending emails, regardless. He wanted to get ahead with his project before the outing tomorrow and have everything in place.

He worked steadily until his stomach alerted him to the fact that it was well past lunchtime, so he stood, stretching out stiff limbs, and walked into the kitchen to prepare something. As he wandered back through into the lounge and onto the terrace, nibbling on some Manchego, he looked out to sea and tried to decide what to do with the rest of his day. With a start, he remembered Father Thomas and his worrying cough, and the fact he hadn't called him yesterday. He put his plate down on the glass-topped wrought-iron table and made the call.

It went straight to voicemail. The sound of the old

man's voice made him smile, and he left a message to say he would call back later. Hearing Father Thomas made him think about the priest's words. Take some time out to enjoy yourself. He pondered this idea as he finished his lunch and decided there was nothing further he could do work-wise right now until people started to respond to his emails, so he was going to go for a swim. Roused by the idea of doing something as simple as spending time on the beach, he finished his lunch eagerly, rinsed his plate, and went to get ready.

CHAPTER ELEVEN

Abi was having an amazingly relaxing day. Stretched out on her beach towel under the canopy of an enormous umbrella the others had brought with them, she watched as the boys played handball, showing off for the girls.

Anya had brought two of her friends with her, lovely girls who, despite her lack of their language, did their best to make her feel included. When they stood to go for a swim, Abi declined the offer for her to go in with them. She had just reapplied her sunscreen and wanted to wait until it had soaked in properly before risking exposing herself to the sun, which was beating down mercilessly.

Anya said something to them and then settled back on her towel. 'You don't have to stay here with me,' Abi said, laughing when the other two squealed as a ball came flying close over their heads.

'It's OK,' Anya replied, smiling at her. 'I'm happy enough here. So, tell me, Abi, how are you settling in?

Are you getting used to the way of life here?'

'I am,' Abi replied, looking happily at her new friend.

'Is there anything you miss from England?'

Abi thought about her old life, her job, her flat and Jason, and it startled her to find that it felt more like a dream than a reality.

'You know, it's funny, when I came here, splitting up with Jason seemed like the biggest calamity of my life, but I can honestly say I haven't thought about him for days.'

She sat up and reached for a bottle of water in the cool box next to them, proffering one to Anya, who took it gratefully. 'What about family?' she asked as she cracked the lid and took a sip.

'Well, there's just dad now, and we don't talk much anymore.'

Anya looked perplexed. 'How can you not talk to your father? I can't imagine such a thing.'

'It's complicated,' Abi replied, looking out at the teal waters and thinking about what May had told her. It had been playing on her mind and tugging at her heartstrings and she didn't know what to do about it.

Anya snorted. 'Of course it is. It's family. It's messy and loud and sometimes incredibly irritating,' she said emphatically with a glance at where Miquel was diving with a bellow onto the sand, hand outstretched to reach the ball. 'But at the end of the day, it's family, and that's what matters.'

Abi nodded in response as a memory popped up unbidden. She must have been four or five, standing on her father's feet as he danced her around the kitchen. Mum sat laughing at the table. His warbling rendition of You are My Sunshine echoing around the room. She felt tears spring up and a pang of loss. Almost fifteen years had passed since she had spent any real time with the man that used to call her his sunshine. Maybe she should give him a chance? Everything her aunt had told her was altogether at odds with how she had perceived the situation as a teenager. Could she have gotten things so wrong? After years of thinking the worst of him, it was hard to adjust.

'I am getting too warm,' Anya pushed herself up with her elbows. 'I'm going for a swim. Are you coming?'

'I'll be there in a minute,' Abi replied, reaching a decision. Shading her eyes as she looked up at her, 'there's something I need to do first.'

As Anya walked towards the sea, Abi got her phone back out of her bag and tried to compose an email to her dad. It took longer than she expected and was even harder than she could have imagined. She typed and deleted the opening paragraph a dozen times before working out what she wanted to say.

In the end, she just opted for a breezy sounding update of her life, letting him know she was here in

Spain with May and telling him a little about the new job she had. Not able to get into the ins and outs of her emotions by such a cold medium as an email. That was definitely a conversation they would have to have face to face. That's if he still wanted anything to do with her after she had knocked back his attempts at repairing their relationship so many times over the years.

The other girls had returned from their swim by the time she was ready to hit the send button. As they approached with the boys who had tired of their game, the discussion was about food, as it was lunch-time.

'We're going to get some wraps from the café,' Miquel said, smiling down at her. 'Do you want to come with us?'

'No thank you, I was just going for a swim. Just grab me something, I don't mind what. I'll keep an eye on our stuff.'

Abi stood up, threw her hat on the towel and headed towards the sea as the others dried off and got their shoes on. As she entered the warm water, she glanced back and saw them walking up the beach towards the café. Turning, she watched the windsurfers skimming across the sea in the distance for a moment before she sank into the inviting blue, and ducked her hair back in the water. She let out a sigh as it cooled her head and she lay there floating for a while. Enjoying the feeling of weightlessness as it rippled around her. She turned and swam a few leisurely strokes before heading back towards the shore. She didn't want to leave their things unattended for too long.

When she reached the shallows, she stood and noticed someone standing by their belongings, staring at her. Shit, it was Gabe, she realised with a start. She'd recognise him anywhere. Suddenly self-conscious in her new bikini, she hesitated, but there was nothing for it but to keep walking. Marching over, she whipped up her towel and wrapped it around her, wishing it was bigger, and retrieved her hat from where it fell, shaking the sand from it before putting it on.

'Hi, Gabe. How are you today?' she asked, eyes looking anywhere but at his bare chest.

'I'm doing great,' he replied with a smile, lifting his sunglasses and resting them on his head. His eyes were unashamedly roaming her body, barely covered by the beach towel. Feeling herself flush yet again, she bent to get some more water from the cool box.

'Decided to take a swim?' she gestured with the bottle at his shorts before taking a drink, trying to ignore his well-muscled legs.

'Seems to be a popular choice today,' he replied, looking around. The beach was getting busier, dotted with groups of people, splashes of brilliantly coloured towels peppering the golden sand, umbrellas ruffling in the slight breeze. 'So, I decided I'd come and see what the attraction was.' His gaze settled back on her face, dark blue eyes so intent and unfathomable and that damn dimple springing up as he smiled.

Abi heard her phone chime. *Saved by the bell,* she thought as she reached into her bag. It was a request from her next guest, asking her to organise a surprise anniversary dinner for his wife, and she smiled at the sweetness of it.

'Good news?' Gabe inquired, still staring at her avidly.

'Yes. I mean, kind of.' She replied, not wanting to get into this with him and putting her phone away. As she looked back up, she saw the others coming back. 'Ah, here are my friends,' she said with relief. The group converged with excited chatter and greetings, Miquel moving in swiftly to stand almost protectively next to her.

'Here you go, Abi,' he passed her the warm wrap, folded in a napkin. 'It is chorizo and cheese; I hope you like it.' She took it with a smile of thanks, and the others sat down on their towels and unwrapped their lunches, leaving the three of them standing there awkwardly.

'Well,' she looked at Gabe pointedly. 'So, I'll see you tomorrow morning then?'

He slipped his glasses back over his eyes and gave a curt nod. 'Sure thing, Abigail.' He turned and walked off back up the beach, his long strides covering the sand rapidly. Wondering if she had been a bit rude, Abi looked down as Anya burst out laughing at something one of the other girls had said.

'Lisette here said that he's so...' she paused, looking for the word in English. 'Edible, yes, that's it. He's so edible she'd like to put him in her wrap!'

Settling down next to her, Abi couldn't help but laugh along with them. 'She's not wrong. He is rather yummy,' she admitted, earning her a sharp look from Miquel. She had noticed that Lisette kept glancing at Miquel and wondered if the girl had a thing for him, but he seemed oblivious to her presence.

'I think he thinks the same about you,' Anya continued, surprising her. 'The way he stares at you, pretty intense, no?'

A flush of pleasure shot through her at these words, but she said hastily, 'I don't think so, Anya. And anyway, after everything I have been through recently, the last thing I need is a man like Gabe Xavier. He's far too unpredictable.'

'Yes, Abi. You need someone more reliable. And also, he seems a little cold,' Miquel piped up. Abi and Anya exchanged a look as they took the first bites of their lunch. She couldn't help but speculate, though, what it would be like to be with a man like Gabe. Exciting, most likely, her inner voice cried out. Unstable and inevitably heart-breaking, her common sense chimed in as she ate her delicious lunch.

Gabe went to a bar further up the beach, his head buzzing. Why had he gone over? He should have just left her in peace, not opened himself up for that definite dismissal that had left him feeling so bad. He ordered a beer and took a seat on the terrace, consciously turning away from where Abigail was sitting with her friends. God knows what had come over him. This girl had him acting like a teenager, an awkward one at that. The word God reminded him, and he redialled Father Thomas, frowning as it went to voicemail yet again. It wasn't like the old man to have his phone turned off all day.

The temperature was rising, and the water was calling to him, so once he had finished his beer, he claimed a spot on the sand with his towel and strode towards the sea. As the warm water rose to his chest, he surged forward and dived in. It was blissful. He surfaced a few feet on and rolled onto his back, giving a lazy kick to propel him onwards with a bark of laughter. When was the last time he had done something as mindlessly enjoyable as swimming in the ocean?

He lay there, allowing the current to take him where it wanted and his thoughts returned to his life and how barren it was. He wanted to make changes, but wasn't sure how to proceed. Yes, this new project had given him a buzz, but he knew it was going to take more than that to make a radical change to the ennui he had been experiencing in his life.

Looking up, he could see the shore in the distance, so he flipped onto his front and, with powerful strokes, made his way back towards the sand. When he reached the shallows, he stood and couldn't help but look toward Abigail and her friends. He saw her walking towards the water with a bright pink Lilo and smiled at the sight. Rubbing the excess of water from his body with his towel, he then snapped it out back on the sand and lay on it, enjoying the feel of the sunlight on his body.

Gabe found the warmth of the sun soothing and the torrid thoughts that had been torturing him dissipated as he dozed off for a while. His eyes shot open when a passing child squealed in excitement and he looked around, disorientated. How long had he been sleeping? He pushed himself up on his elbows and looked to his left. Yup, Abigail's friends were still there. But where was she? He swivelled his eyes out to the sea and saw to his alarm the splash of pink that had to be her Lilo, way off on the horizon.

He stood, still straining to see how far out she was, and hovered uncertainly for a moment before racing down to the water and diving in. With strong strokes, he pounded through the water. It became colder the further out he got, but he concentrated on one stroke after another. He hadn't swum in a long time and his arms were already protesting at the unusual exertion, but he just focused on reaching that Lilo.

Abi had needed some time to think after lunch,

and had borrowed Anya's Lilo to give herself some space. As she bobbed along her mind was a tumult of concerns. Would her dad respond to her email? Could they repair the damage to their relationship, especially now she was in another country? And why did Gabe Xavier look so damn fine in his swimming trunks? She closed her eyes against the glare of the sun, her lids saturated with an unfamiliar orange glow as she drifted off to sleep and out to sea.

A splash of cold water and the Lilo dipping alarmingly at one end was the first she was aware of her plight. Lifting her head in shock, she saw Gabe, arms resting on the inflatable, head bowed and panting before she understood with horror how far out she was. The beach was way off in the distance. She could scarcely make it out.

'Oh my God,' she cried, looking about in panic. 'I must have drifted off to sleep.'

'I figured as much,' he expelled between ragged breaths, still managing a wry grin. 'That's why I did my Baywatch impression.'

He gave a kick of his legs and laboured to turn the ungainly Lilo around so he could propel it back towards the shore and safety. His arms were now too tired to do anything but clutch the slippery plastic as best they could. It was slow progress until Abi slipped off into the water and came next to him and added her efforts to his without a word. When they eventually reached the shallows, they lay at the water's edge.

Gabe exhausted from his efforts, Abi still in shock at the precarious position she had let herself get into.

'Gabe,' she said finally, as the water lapped gently around them. 'How can I ever thank you?'

He glanced over at her; his eyes drawn to the water beading down her neck towards her breasts. 'Don't mention it,' he looked at her with a smile that made her heart beat even faster than the adrenaline rush of danger minutes ago. 'I'm sure someone would have spotted you, soon or later.'

'I'm not so sure,' she looked around at the groups of people along the beach, happily getting on with their day. 'Seems like I would be halfway across the Bay of Biscay if it wasn't for you.'

She reached out the hand that wasn't holding the Lilo and touched his shoulder. A shiver ran down her arm, goosebumps pitting the length of it. She stared at it in surprise, as if it wasn't a part of her. When she looked up, Gabe's eyes were studying her face keenly, his dark blue eyes probing every detail. They were just inches apart, and she leaned forward, desperately drawn towards him as she saw his gaze drop to her lips.

'Abi! Are you OK?' Miquel shouted, arriving next to them at a run and stumbling to a stop with a shower of sand. The sound of his voice was like a bucket of cold water being thrown over the scene, and she jerked away from Gabe with a start. She pushed herself up onto her knees and smiled up at him.

'I'm fine, Miquel. I dropped off to sleep, but luckily Gabe here spotted me and came to my rescue.'

Casting a glare at the hero, Miquel said, 'well, I'm just happy you are alright.' And bent to pull the Lilo out of the water for her. She stood and looked down at Gabe. His eyes were unwavering, but his face was impassive now.

'Look, can I buy you a drink or something?' she said in pleading tones. 'I honestly can't thank you enough.'

His eyes flicked ever so briefly to the bristling young man next to her before he replied. 'Some other time maybe.' He stood up next to them, water cascading down his muscled body, drawing attention to every dip and contour. Abi stared, mesmerised, hardly hearing his words as he continued.
'I need to get back. I have business to attend to and calls to make.'

He looked at her expectantly, the growing silence pulling her out of her trance. 'Oh, OK. Well, I guess I will see you in the morning then?' she said with a dawning realisation that tomorrow seemed like too far away.

'You certainly will.' There was a glint in his eye, and with a brief wave, he walked back up the beach to his towel.

'Come on, Abi,' Miquel put an arm around her shoulder. 'Let's get you back.' Obediently allowing him to steer her towards the others, she couldn't help glancing back wistfully at Gabe.

She had been trying so hard to brush off the growing attraction she felt toward him, but now? Would she be able to ignore it when she had to spend a whole day with him tomorrow? She was beginning to think it was an impossible task.

CHAPTER TWELVE

The next morning, Abi was awake before dawn and crept into the kitchen to make her coffee, hoping not to disturb her aunt. But she had forgotten about Bob, whose head popped out from under his wing as soon as he heard the machine start to pump its elixir.

'Morning, May! Morning, May!' he screeched happily, bobbing up and down on his perch and flapping his wings.

'Shh, you stupid bird,' she whispered at him sharply, but he just continued to dance up and down the branch, his cries getting louder by the minute. May appeared a few moments later, her hair wild and medusa-like, her expression befuddled.

'What time is it?' she looked at Abi with unfocused, sleepy eyes.

'I'm sorry, May. It's still early. Why don't you go back to bed?'

May shook her head and shuffled over to the coffee machine. 'No, I'm up now. Early nerd catches the worm and all that. I wanted to be up early today, anyway.'

The sun was just peeping over the rooftops as they went out onto the balcony, the air still cool from the night. They sat in silence for a while, enjoying the peace and watching the brilliant orange rays of the sun wash over the buildings before them as it rose. May turned to look at Abi and let out a braying laugh that rang out across the street and bounced off the buildings opposite.

'What?' Abi demanded. 'What the hell is so funny?' perplexed at what could amuse her aunt so much at this time of the morning.

'Have you looked in the mirror yet today?' her aunt asked with glee. 'I think you forgot to put sun cream on your nose. You look like Rudolph!' Abi's hand flew to her face as May continued to giggle. It felt sensitive, damn it. How on earth had that happened? She had been so careful with applying protection and wearing her hat. With a start, she realised that it must have been when she had drifted out to sea and fallen asleep.

Gabe flashed into her mind, water dripping down his sculpted body, his piercing blue eyes looking deep into hers, his lips tantalisingly inviting. Abi shook her head, trying to dislodge the image as she ran to the bathroom to inspect the damage. She looked at her glowing nose with a cry of dismay. *It looks ridiculous,* she thought as she applied a large dollop of after-sun to it. May was still giggling when she came back outside.

'Well, I'm glad you find it amusing,' she huffed as she sat back down.

'Oh, Abi, dear. It did make me giggle. I'm sorry. But don't worry, I'm sure I have something that will help cover it up.'

'Thanks, May,' she said over the rim of her cup. 'It was my own silly fault, I guess,' she gave her aunt a wry smile. The two of them continued to talk for a while, only pausing to get some pastries and more coffee from the kitchen and enjoying their leisurely morning together. When the church bells down the street chimed the hour, Abi jumped up from her seat. 'I'd better get a move on, May.' She bolted the last of her pastry and took a final swig of coffee.

'We're taking the orphans out today.'

'Well, that should be fun,' her aunt said. 'Shall we meet up for dinner? I plan on painting all day today, so I'll need to get out of the apartment later.'

'That sounds perfect,' replied Abi, and hurried to get dressed. She gave a last, mournful glance at her singed nose before she left, tutting at her reflection. She had done her best with the concealer May had given her, but it was still glaringly obvious.

Gabe had woken up at a ridiculous time, too. He had stayed in his bed for about an hour to try to get back to sleep, but it was no good. He gave up trying and roused himself to make some coffee, before walking out to the terrace and watching the sunrise contemplatively.

Today was an important day for his plans, he couldn't afford to be distracted. The incident with Abi yesterday kept playing across his mind and it was driving him crazy. He had desperately wanted to kiss her. And he was pretty sure she had felt the same way before that damn barman had come along to disturb them. He stood up abruptly. He was going to have to get his brain back on track and sitting here thinking about her would not do that.

He showered and dressed in smart blue slacks and a crisp white shirt. Looking at his reflection, he smiled. *That's better*, he thought. Business-like, no-nonsense, more like his usual self. Cool, calm, Gabe had been restored. As it was still early, he opened up his MacBook and settled down to do some work. It was only when he heard church bells chiming the hour that he looked back up. She'd be here soon. Butterflies appeared from nowhere in his stomach, causing him to frown. He was going to have to make a concerted effort to keep focused today and not let Abigail Johnson distract him.

Abi was all a jitter as she waited at the meeting

point for Gabe and the minibus, her fingers tapping out a nervous tattoo on her thighs, and her mind was all over the place. She saw the sleek, black bus approaching as she heard the sound of his voice. She turned and saw him striding towards her, phone clamped to his ear, barking commands at some poor soul on the other end of the line. He looked gorgeous, his shirt fitting his frame perfectly, and she couldn't help but think about what she knew was underneath it. The bus's doors opened with a hiss, and the driver called out a cheery greeting.

'*Buenos días,*' he called, 'Abi?' She nodded and smiled, turning to wait for Gabe to finish up his call, but he barely glanced at her and just climbed the steps onto the bus without a break in his conversation.

'I need you to get this completed today, Marianna,' he was saying as he sat in the single seat at the front of the bus, leaving Abi to pick a seat somewhere else. She sat behind the driver, feeling bereft. He seemed so cold and distant this morning. She leaned forward and confirmed to the driver their destination, then sat back, gazing unseeing out the window as they drove out of town.

'Everything OK?' she asked when he finally finished his call.

'Yes, fine, just some business I needed to attend to.'

There was a strained silence as the bus wended its way through the morning rush hour, which continued as they hit the open road. It was only as they approached the orphanage and the protesters came into view that he spoke again.

'What's going on there?' he asked with a frown as he took in the scene.

'Oh, we are fighting against some bigwig property developer who is trying to buy the nature reserve,' she looked over, glad of the conversation. He watched the protesters as they drove past with a speculative look on his face.

'You said "we". Are you involved in that?'

'Oh, yes,' she said proudly. 'In fact, we have a big media event planned for tomorrow to raise awareness.'

He looked at her sharply but kept his lips tightly pressed together as the bus pulled up in front of the rambling building that was the orphanage. Stepping out of the bus, she could see, now she was paying attention, that the building was falling apart. Drain pipes were sagging, paint was peeling off all the window frames, and it had the overall air of a building long abandoned.

The front door opened, and a dark-haired woman walked out, closing the door behind her and smiling at them as she came down the steps.

'Good morning, I am Jakinda. I am in charge here,' she introduced herself to Gabe, shaking both their hands cordially. 'Thank you so much for doing this. The children are very excited, they don't get trips out often, so they may be a little, how would you say, hyper?'

Abi smiled at the thought. 'That's totally fine,' she said. 'Shall we get them on the bus?'

Jakinda nodded and hurried back up the steps to open the door. A stream of children rushed out, chattering excitedly and piling onto the bus, fighting over which seats they would have. All except one small boy, who stood quietly behind Jakinda, looking solemnly on. Jakinda crouched down and spoke to him softly. He nodded at what she had said, and as she stood back up, he took her hand and she led him onto the bus.

'Shall we?' Abi looked at Gabe, who was staring, sadly, after the boy with an expression she couldn't fathom. As they got back on the bus, Jakinda called out, 'we just have to wait for Paula, my assistant, and then we can be off.' Looking out of the window, Abi could see a small, older woman just locking up the door and, once she was on and settled in her seat, they started the journey back into town.

Whatever had been bugging Gabe earlier seemed to have passed, and he was soon in deep conversation with Jakinda. Firing all sorts of questions at her about the funding for the orphanage, the building itself, and their horror at the possibility that a building site was soon going to be covering what was essentially the kids' playground.

When the bus pulled up in town, Abi stood and announced with a smile, 'Right, girls and boys. Our first stop is going to be Dooers Sneakers, as I've been told your feet grow too fast!' She waited while Jakinda translated this, and the cheers and giggles that greeted this told her it had been a good choice.

She led the way along the narrow street, through the shoppers, the kids following eagerly behind her in pairs, watched carefully by the orphanage staff. When she got to the door of the shop, she knocked on it. She had called ahead and arranged a private shopping hour for them, figuring it would be easier to control things if there weren't other customers in there fighting for attention.

The staff in the store were brilliant with the children and soon had them organised, measuring their feet before helping them choose. The walls were a colourful display of every brand of trainers you could think of, and squeals of delight echoed around the shop as they made each discovery. Abi smiled, looking around until she spotted Gabe. He was crouched down in front of the small boy, who had seemed reluctant to get on the bus earlier. The boy was sitting on one of the stools, Paula next to him translating what Gabe was saying.

Abi walked over in time to see the boy gradually stretch out an arm and point at a pair of red trainers. Gabe walked over and held one up questioningly. The little boy nodded, a tiny smile appearing on his solemn face. Gabe collard one of the staff, who went scurrying to the back room, and soon reappeared with a box. She stood next to Gabe while the boy tried them on, standing up as instructed and marching proudly up and down to test them.

'Didn't he want to get some shoes?' Abi asked, looking at Gabe who was grinning at the boy.

'Oh, he did. Diego just didn't believe it was actually happening,' he glanced at her, then back at the boy. 'It happens when kids have been let down one time too many. They lose faith in adults.'

She examined his face. There was something in his tone that suggested he knew what he was talking about, but his expression gave nothing away. He returned her gaze with a smile that made her heart flutter alarmingly.

'So, what's next on the agenda?' he asked, looking around and seeing that most of the kids seemed to be flaunting their new footwear to each other.

'Well, once we have finished here, I have arranged for a trip to the aquarium. I thought it might be fun for them.'

'That sounds like it might be fun for all of us,' he laughed. 'It's been a while since the last time I did something like that.'

Thrilled that he was happy with her idea, Abi went to check with Jakinda that everyone had their purchases, and she had to organise several bags to take away the old ones as all the children wanted to wear their new shoes. While Gabe paid the bill, she called the driver to come back around and meet them, and they shepherded the gaggle of excited children back to the bus.

It was just a short drive to the aquarium, perched on the seawall in the old port, but the volume of noise from the kids had reached a crescendo as they pulled up. Paula stood and gave them what must have been a stern talking to, as they were soon quietly getting off the bus and lining up in pairs by the stairs. The guide, a serious young woman with large glasses, met them by the door and introduced herself, then explained a little about the history of the place before they went in.

Fidgeting as they listened to her talk about the exhibits chronicling the city's maritime history, it was only when they came to the aquarium proper that the children began to take an interest and pepper the guide with questions. Gabe fell into step with Abi as they wandered around, admiring the sea life on display. She stopped in front of the tank housing a colony of seahorses, mesmerised by their delicate, bobbing forms.

'They look so fragile,' she bent down to examine them more closely. 'They're incredible.'

'Seahorses mate for life, you know?' Gabe said, watching her face, lit up by the lights of the tank. She turned her head slightly and looked up at him.

'Really?'

'Yup, they do. And it's said that if one of the pair

dies, the remaining one goes into decline, sometimes they even die. It's like they're heartbroken.'

Standing back up, she looked at him curiously. 'You seem to know a lot about them.'

'I spent a lot of time hanging around the aquarium back home when I was a kid. Sometimes I still go there now, when I need to think.' He was staring at the tank but seeing something else entirely.
'I was abandoned as a baby,' he twisted to look at her. 'I grew up in an orphanage. That's why I wanted to do this,' he said, gesturing around at the kids running joyfully from one exhibit to another.

'Oh, Gabe. That's horrible,' she reached out and touched his arm.

'It was pretty awful,' he said. 'Although the staff at the orphanage were great. I'm still excellent friends with Father Thomas who runs it.'

He looked so lost, so unlike his usual cocky self, that she instinctively moved in to hug him. The warmth from his body seeped into hers and she shifted in closer, snuggly fitting to his form as he haltingly raised his arms to return the embrace. Her head on his chest, she could feel his heart racing, its rhythm matching the pounding of the blood in her veins. What had been an instinctive gesture to comfort him producing an explosion of fireworks in her body. She was fizzing all over.

Abi looked up into his handsome face and he deliberately lowered his head and placed the gentlest kiss on her lips. Everything faded away; the chatter of the children, the weird flickering glow of the room, as her whole being focused on that one sensation. Time seemed to stand still and Abi was lost in the moment. When he moved away slightly, her eyes sprang open, and reality came flooding back. He looked as startled as she felt, and they moved apart swiftly. Jakinda came bustling over as the children swarmed past them, their voices echoing around the room.

'They have heard about the sharks in the tunnel over there,' she said, laughing as she pointed after the kids. 'I think it is more exciting than the shoes,' she grinned and hurried after the disappearing group.

'We'd better follow them,' he said quickly and turned in the tunnel's direction. Abigail stood for a moment, staring after him, collecting her thoughts together. *What the hell had just happened*? She touched her lips in wonder. They were still fizzing from his kiss. Excited shrieks up ahead got her moving, and she followed the noise and walked into the glass tunnel. Momentarily awed by the sight of sharks swimming overhead, it took a second before she realised there was no sign of Gabe. Paula, seeing her look around, came over and said, 'he's gone out to make a phone call. There's no signal in here.'

Gabe had indeed gone outside, but not because he needed a signal. What he needed was some fresh air and a chance to think. He did not know why he'd felt the urge to tell Abigail about his childhood. The urge to kiss her was more obvious. She was gorgeous, despite her sunburnt nose, and impossible to ignore when she had held him so tightly. It was going to make things a little awkward, though. He shook his head at his foolishness. So much for staying professional today.

He waited outside and took out his phone and checked his emails. Reading the latest one from Marianna, he smiled and punched the air. The deal was closed! The rush of pleasure he felt at this new venture planted a seed of hope in himself. Maybe he could open up to other new possibilities after all.

CHAPTER
THIRTEEN

When Abi and the others came outside, they found Gabe leaning against the wall, grinning like a Cheshire cat. Her heart started pounding at the mere sight of him and she took a few deep calming breaths, hoping that it would regulate her body's absurd reaction. She was still reeling from the kiss. Her mind just could not take on board what had happened, but her body seemed to have no such qualms and her stomach was doing excited somersaults.

'So, gang, did we enjoy that?' he asked expansively, looking to Jakinda to relay the question, which she did swiftly. The whoops and cheers from the children resoundingly answered him and his smile widened even further.

'Well, I think it's time for some lunch, don't you?' he looked at Abi for the first time. She nodded with a weak smile and looked around for the bus. Seeing it parked a little further up the street, she set off in that direction, her mind still a jumble of thoughts. She couldn't believe he had kissed her, and more importantly, she couldn't believe she had let him. The fact that she had enjoyed it so much was something else she would have to think about later.

The restaurant she had chosen was called La Perla Bar Restaurante. It overlooked La Concha beach, the swathe of golden sand the city was famous for. A large table on the terrace was waiting for them, which was soon awash with clamorous chatter, plates of pintxos, and drinks all around. The children were in seventh heaven, stuffing their faces and taking large gulps of the Coca-Colas or juices they had chosen.

Gabe was sitting at the far end of the table, talking with Jakinda, and Abi watched him from her seat next to Paula. He looked happy, unconcerned by what had happened at the aquarium. Maybe it had meant nothing to him? *He probably goes around kissing random women all the time* her inner voice taunted her.

Abigail was in turmoil, barely able to touch her food. Her efforts at ignoring the undeniable attraction she had towards him had been blown away by the merest brush of his lips. The sound of chairs scraping back noisily made her glance up. The children were up and running towards the beach, supervised by the two women from the orphanage. Even in her distracted state, she smiled at the sight of their boisterous departure.

Gabe, who was feeling buoyant at today's success, came over and sat next to her.

'This has all been perfect,' he smiled at her. 'Thank you so much. I couldn't have asked for a better day for them.' He looked across to where the kids were paddling in the shallows. Their new shoes were abandoned in a colourful pile on the sand.

'They certainly seem to be enjoying it,' Abi replied, watching his dimple flex as he smiled at the scene. When he turned to look at her, his face was intent and his eyes serious. Her insides twisted as she returned his gaze, wondering what was on his mind.

'Abigail, I'd like you to book a restaurant for tonight.'

Her stomach lurched in disappointment. She had been so sure he was going to say, or maybe do, something else entirely. Certainly not ask for a dinner reservation.

'OK, no problem. Where would you like to go?' she twisted around to pull her notebook out of her bag hanging on the back of the chair. She placed it on her lap and, pen poised, looked up at him, fronds of hair falling across her face. He reached out and tucked one of them gently behind her ear.

'Where would you suggest for a first date?' he asked, the sly grin returning. Abi could feel the flush rising to her cheeks as his words sank in, and she stared helplessly into his eyes.

'Are you talking about me?' she uttered, her mind racing.

'I am,' he confirmed. 'I think we should spend some more time together. What do you think?' An unfamiliar flash of uncertainty crossed his face. She sat back a little, trying to work out what to do. She would like nothing more than to spend time with him. Her heart raced at the prospect. But this was her job, and he would be leaving in a couple of days. Was there any point?

'I'm not sure that's a good idea,' she said finally, almost laughing at the surprise on his face. Gabe Xavier was not used to women saying no to him. He glanced up at the sound of the children returning, the promise of ice cream causing them to run eagerly back to their seats.

'Well, at least think about it?' he asked quietly, gazing at her steadily. She gave a slight nod in response as Jakinda walked up to ask her about the bus to return to the orphanage and the moment was lost.

Leaning against the window as she accompanied them back home, Abigail let the sounds of the bus wash over her as she looked out at the passing landscape. Her mind replayed the conversation with Gabe at lunch. He had chosen to walk back to the apartment when they had finished at the restaurant, but not before every single child had hugged him ferociously to show their thanks. He had looked quite emotional as he tried to brush away their gratitude. She was sure he had tears in his eyes when he turned to walk away.

There seemed to be another side to this man. The cold, hard business image he liked to present to the world was just a shield, covering something else entirely. What he had told her about his childhood was awful. She was sure there was more to uncover. She'd had a pretty rough time of it, but at least she knew her parents had loved her. That made her think of her father. She'd been trying not to dwell on the fact that he hadn't replied to her email yet.

She waved off the children with promises to visit them soon and told Jakinda about tomorrow's planned media coverage to stop the property development. The woman was painfully grateful and eagerly promised to rouse up as many supporters as she could for the event.

The driver chatted away to her on the way back to town, but her mind was elsewhere. Her muted responses didn't deter him, though, and she soon knew his entire life story. She nodded in all the right places, wishing he would shut up. *I need to talk to someone about all this,* she thought, and she knew just who the right person was.

By mutual consent, Abi and her aunt went to Baztan Pintxos & Bar for dinner, but she waited until they were seated and Miquel had taken their orders before she broached the subject of Gabe. Aunt May listened attentively, a small smile on her face, while her niece poured out her heart. Describing their day together, the fleeting kiss and his suggestion that they go on a date.

'So, what's the problem?' May was gnawing on a breadstick, then waved it around as she said, 'there's no harm going on a date, surely?'

'That's just it. There's plenty of harm. Firstly, he is a client, my first one to boot. I'm not sure of the protocol, but I feel sure Sublime Retreats would frown on me fraternising with guests. Secondly, well, what's the point?'

'The point, Abi dear, is that you are allowed to have a little fun, and who knows where this will lead? You can't let worry about work or what it means in the long run stop you from taking a chance. Look at me and Pedro. I work with him, but I still took the leap. Yes, it might not work out, but I am having a fine time being romanced, so I don't care.'

'I don't have your easy-going outlook on life, May. I worry about the future. What surprises are around the corner...' she trailed off. Miquel, who had been serving them, put a hand on her shoulder.

'If it's worth anything, I think you are right to hold back. I don't trust that man, and it would be a shame to do anything to put your new job at risk,' he said seriously, looking at her intently, a strange expression etched on his face, before returning to the bar.

'You see? I'm not the only one who thinks it's a mistake!' She flapped out her napkin and lay it on her lap.

'Pish,' retorted May, as she picked up her cutlery. 'I love that young man, but he's just jealous and wants you for himself. Pay no mind to his opinion when it comes to matters of your heart.'

They ate in silence for a while, Abi still in two minds about what to do, torn between her heart and her usual common sense.

'By the way,' May said suddenly with a grin. 'I got a call from the gallery today. All but four of my paintings have sold.'

'That's fantastic news,' Abi replied, Gabe forgotten for a moment. 'Congratulations,' she raised her wineglass at her.

'Congratulations to you too, my dear. It's because of your excellent planning that it was such a success. That reminds me, is everything set for tomorrow at the protest?'

'I think so. Anya has organised for some friends of hers who are in a band to come and play. They have quite a big following, so that should get the crowds out, and I have called on Pedro's cousin at the paper to come and cover the event.' She looked pensive for a second, 'I'm hoping it will cause enough of a splash to get picked up by the National's, then we will definitely have some attention.'

Her aunt shook her head, marvelling at her niece's

ingenuity. 'That sounds amazing and fun. And I still think you should go out with Mr Unusual, even if it's just to get him out of your system!'

As if he had heard her aunt's words, a text came through from Gabe.

Have you thought about it?

Smiling at the timing, Abi weighed up her options. The pros and cons circled her mind like hungry sharks. She knew May was right, she should take more chances in life. After her mum had died, she had worked hard at building a safe, dependable life, always choosing the rational option and ignoring any impulses with well-reasoned arguments. She didn't want any more surprises; they were usually unpleasant. But where had taking the safe, sensible option got her so far? With a feckless fiancée, jobless, and then homeless, all in the space of a few weeks.

Before she could change her mind, she typed her response with shaking fingers.

We could go for a walk?

Gabe, who had been a nervous bag of energy since he had got back to the apartment, looked at the message with delight. A walk; that was a start, right? He quickly replied to say he would meet her by the carousel in half an hour and quickly went to change out of his business clothes. A quick sniff of his armpits confirmed his fears. He was a bit ripe after all his nervous pacing. He rushed into the bathroom and stood under the pulsing jets of the shower for a few moments, zealously washing before leaping out, grabbing a towel to rub down with as he raced back up the hallway.

He arrived at the meeting point five minutes early and found her already waiting there for him, the lights from the carousel lighting up her face in the dusk. He took a moment to study her, still not entirely sure why this woman affected him so deeply to the point where he couldn't stop thinking about her.

'Hey,' he said softly, smiling at her as he approached.

'Hey, yourself,' she replied breathlessly, and they stood staring at each other. 'Well, this is awkward,' she looked away and watched the children getting off the ride.

Gabe had to agree; he hadn't thought this through. He didn't usually need to. Following her gaze to the gleeful children getting off the carousel, he grabbed her hand impulsively. 'Come on,' he said and pulled her towards it.

'You can't possibly expect me to get on this thing?' she laughed as they reached the ride.

'I can and I do. In fact, I insist!' he said firmly, stepping up and pulling her on with him. Finding herself unable to resist, she looked around and climbed on a dainty white horse with a dark red saddle, a radiant smile on her face. Throwing his leg over the steed next to her, he tried to put his feet on the footrests, but this forced his long legs to bend up impossibly high, so he settled for holding them aloft. Children swarmed on around them, giggling at the sight of these crazy adults, but soon the tinny music began and it started to turn.

With each revolution, Abi felt the stress of the last few days leave her body and she leant back, clutching the pole for support, her red hair streaming out behind her. Gabe looked across at her, bathed in the glow of the flashing-coloured lights. She looked so carefree and so beautiful, his mouth dried up as longing swept through his body. Not just the physical, although that was certainly there. But a longing for a life where he could jump on a carousel with someone special and just enjoy the moment.

When it finally came to a halt, they climbed off laughing. 'I can't believe we just did that,' she said as they walked towards the beach, nudging him playfully with her shoulder. He nudged her back, grinning from ear to ear.

'Trust me, if anyone who knew me had seen me do that, they wouldn't have believed it either.'

They walked along in easy silence for a moment, moving out of the way of families heading towards the carousel, and stepped down onto the soft sand. Strolling along the beach, they were both lost in their own worlds. Gabe wondering how this woman had broken down his defences so easily and grateful that her reluctance to spend time with him seemed to have abated. Abi was marvelling at the fact she was technically on a date and still floating from the buzz of the carousel ride. As they approached the end of La Concha, she heard the rattle of the ancient funicular as a carriage carried its passengers up the hill. She placed her hand on his arm. 'Gabe, can we go up there?'

He looked to see where she was pointing to and a smile reappeared as he nodded.

'Race ya!' she cried impulsively and set off across the last of the sand and up onto the pavement towards the ticket office. He stared, bemused for a second before charging after her, laughter spilling from his lips as he levelled with her and his long strides soon carrying him ahead.

He had to put out his hands to stop himself from crashing into the building. He turned, still laughing as she barrelled into him, panting. His arms wrapped around her to steady her as she recovered from the mad dash and they stood there, out of breath, looking into each other's eyes for what seemed like an eternity.

Abi's blood was pounding through her veins, and not just because of the sprint across the sand. She pulled herself from his embrace but took his hand, not wanting to lose that contact.

'Let's get our tickets,' she said, pulling him towards the door and into the ticket hall. The faded jade-green tiles and over-painted wrought ironwork inside instantly made it feel like they were stepping back in time. Only a few people were waiting in line at the cashier, who called to them as they entered.

'Hurry, if you want to go up, this is the last one of the day.'

Gabe let go of Abi's hand to pull out some cash from his pocket for the tickets, but immediately grabbed it again once he had them. She looked down at their hands in amazement. This should feel weird, right? But it didn't, not by a long shot. Strangely, it felt like the most natural thing in the world. They walked up the steps to the front of the wooden funicular and took their seats on the hard bench just as it lurched to life.

She grinned at him, 'this is turning into quite the adventure, isn't it?'

'This is the most fun I have had in I don't know how long,' he replied, glancing ahead as the carriage lurched to one side. It had come to a split in the tracks, a short loop where the down carriage could pass, and they could see the front of the approaching carriage, its faded red paint emblazoned with the Coca-Cola logo. A group of children leaning out of the windows waved at them. Abi returned their cheerful smiles with a wave of her own as it passed by. Trees surrounded the track and they could glimpse the beach below through the greenery, but that didn't prepare them for the view from the top after the brief journey.

They walked up the steps to the exit and were immediately drawn to a viewing point that looked out over the bay and the expanse of San Sebastian. Abi took a sharp breath at the beauty of it.

'Oh, my,' she whispered, Gabe squeezed her hand in acknowledgement.

'Come on. We only have half an hour before the last ride back down according to the timetable,' he said, and they made their way through the cavernous tunnel and out to the park on the other side. They wandered around, still holding hands, admiring the views from the hilltop. Even at this time of evening, it was spectacular. Pausing to watch the children enjoying the rides at the small funfair, Gabe asked with a grin, 'fancy another ride?'

She laughed. 'I think we shall have to leave that for another day. We're running out of time and I don't particularly want to have to walk all the way back down.'

'Fair enough,' he answered. He leaned in and gave her a kiss, taking a moment to savour it before saying, 'thank you, Abi.'

'Thanks for what?' she asked when she had caught her breath from the bolt of electricity that had run through her at the touch of his lips.

'For meeting me tonight. I wasn't expecting to have so much fun on this trip.'

'Why else would you come here if not to have some

fun?' she queried with a frown as a shout came from the station announcing the last trip back down the hill. They jogged over and joined the tourists, squeezing through the turnstile and climbing on board. It was crowded, so they didn't speak, just nudged each other occasionally, both with silly grins on their faces.

With a final lurch and a squeal of breaks, they arrived back at the seafront and followed the line of people out onto the street and walked back down to the beach.

'So, how long have you been here?' he asked as they strolled along the sand.

'Just a few weeks,' Abi replied. 'It has been lovely to catch up with my aunt. I hadn't seen her for...' she blew a breath through her lips. 'Well, let's just say I haven't seen her for too long. I am beginning to realise the importance of family.' She stopped in her tracks, 'God, I'm sorry, Gabe, I didn't think.'

He shook his head and smiled. 'Don't worry about it, Abigail.'

As they walked along, she thought about what it must be like to grow up with no parents, no family to speak of. It was impossible for her to imagine.

'So, tell me more about your childhood,' she ventured, wanting to understand more about this man.

He hesitated for just a beat, before saying, 'well, as I told you earlier, they abandoned me as a baby. In front of a church, as it happens. Francis Xavier church, to be precise.'

'Xavier? As in your name?'

'Yes, Father Thomas is many things, but original is not one of them,' he said with a warm smile. 'So, Gabe Francis Xavier it is.'

'Where did the Gabe come from?'

'It means the hero of God, I'm told. He always said I was going to do great things.'

'He sounds like a wise man,' she said, stopping and looking up at him. 'Look at what you did for those kids today. That was pretty heroic.'

He laughed dismissively. 'That was nothing. Throwing the money I have at one day out is peanuts, I could do so much more.' He gazed out to sea where the moon's reflection was bobbing in the water. 'What about you? What sort of childhood did you have?' he asked, gesturing for her to sit. She sank onto the sand, stretching her legs out in front of her, and he settled in beside her.

'I was lucky, I suppose,' she replied. 'I grew up in a normal house, with loving parents. It was great… Until it wasn't.' She looked pensive, her eyes bright with tears, and Gabe put his arm around her and pulled her close.

'You don't have to talk about it if you don't want to,' he breathed, leaning his head against hers. Bolstered by his support, she told her tale. Slowly at first, and then gushing out of her as if it had been waiting for this moment, this man. Abi told him everything, even the part about Jason cheating on her and the fact he was now expecting a baby.

'So, that's why I'm here,' she finished up. 'San Sebastian seemed like my best choice, although in hindsight I may have been running away,' she chuckled in the dark. He took hold of her chin and turned her face towards him.

'I, for one, am thrilled that you decided to run away,' he smiled and bent his head to kiss her.
This wasn't the gentle, fleeting kiss of earlier at the aquarium. This was an urgent, searching kiss that had her head spinning and her body responding in a rush of effervescent excitement.

When they pulled apart, she could see lust clouding his eyes. The blue was foggy now as he stared at her with desire, and she felt a pulse of pleasure.

'We're not getting much walking done,' she joked.

'It's overrated,' he smiled. 'Sitting on the sand should get more kudos.'

And so they sat. And they kissed, and they talked until the moon had passed overhead and a faint orangey-red glow appeared on the horizon, alerting the world to the approaching day. Abi couldn't remember ever being so comfortable with someone. She had never shared herself so openly and honestly with another soul. She had always kept a little part of her back, not wanting to open up for fear of being let down, abandoned, and having her trust betrayed. But with Gabe, it seemed like the most natural thing in the world.

CHAPTER FOURTEEN

A church bell in the distance rang out, proclaiming the early hour, and with a start, Abigail realised she had to go. She pulled away, missing the warmth of Gabe's body immediately and deeply, her lips felt bruised and adored.

'I have to go, Gabe, I've got this big thing organised for the protest today.' She stood up, brushing the sand off the back of her legs. He got up and pulled her in for another soul-searching kiss, causing her knees to buckle and her head to spin.

'About that,' he said when they finally broke apart. 'There's something I have to tell you.'

His phone rang, the sound shrill and alien in the pre-dawn quiet of the beach. He pulled it out of his pocket and looked at the screen in surprise. It was the middle of the night back home.

'Hey, what's up?' he answered, gesturing to Abi that he would only be a minute. She watched as he listened to what was being said and saw all the colour drain from his face in an instant.

He ended the call with a curt, 'thanks for letting me know,' turning to her with unseeing eyes.

'Gabe, what's wrong?' she asked swiftly, alarmed by the change in him. Even in this half-light, she could see his face was etched with dread.

'I have to go. I need to make some urgent calls. But we'll catch up later?'

All the warmth from the last few hours had disappeared, and she was at a loss for how to respond as he turned away. She muttered, 'OK then,' to his retreating back as he jogged up the beach without a backward glance. Standing for a moment, Abi wasn't sure what to think. She thought she had met someone worth opening up to, despite her fears, and the last few hours had been blissful as he seemed to feel the same. But now a seed of doubt firmly implanted itself as she walked home. If he could change so mercurially, was she just putting her heart at risk again?

There was no point in going to bed, so when she got back to the apartment, Abi put on the coffee and set out the pastries she had bought at a small bakery along the way. She looked at them for a moment, but her stomach was tied up in knots. There was no way she could eat right now.

'Good morning, sweetheart,' May called from the doorway. 'Oh good, croissants,' she came in, plucking the largest from the plate and taking a bite. 'So, how was last night?' she asked with a knowing grin, the effect slightly ruined by the flakes and crumbs surrounding her mouth. 'I see your bed hasn't been slept in.'

'Don't get too excited, we just talked,' Abi said as she made their coffee. 'But it was... unusual,' she laughed a little, despite her growing sense of unease at how things had ended.

'I should hope so!' May replied, taking the proffered cup and walking out to the balcony. As she sat, she saw Abi's expression. 'Why the long face, then?'

'I don't know, May. It was wonderful. We talked for hours. I felt so comfortable with him, so close. But at the end, he just changed. It was like the Gabe I was getting to know switched off. He got a phone call and went racing off as if I was the least important thing in the world.'

'Well, it must have been something serious, darling. I wouldn't take it personally.'

Abi nodded, but it was hard. She had finally found someone she could open up to, someone who lit up her insides with just a kiss, and it was terrifying. When he had walked away, all her fears had come crashing back around her and she felt like a gawky teenager again.

'Anyway, I have this protest to galvanise. I will not muck this up worrying about Gabe,' she declared bravely.

'That's the spirit,' her aunt said through a mouthful of croissant. 'Let's go stick it to the man!'

There was a good crowd already when they got to the protest. The usual faces were there, plus plenty of new ones. The band had arrived and Abi went over and introduced herself.

'Thanks for doing this,' she said to the lead singer. The young girl smiled. 'It's no problem. It's for a good cause. Where do you want us to set up?' Scoping out the area, Abi pointed over to a patch of grass that was slightly elevated. 'There would be good, I think.'

More people were arriving all the time. Mini-buses pulled up depositing groups of youngsters, who no doubt had come to hear the band, but also older, more intent-looking people. Pedro arrived, pulling May in for a long kiss that left her giggling like a schoolgirl.

'Good morning, Abi,' he greeted her with a warm smile. 'It looks like we will have a good turnout,' he looked around at the amassing crowd.

'It's shaping up pretty well,' she agreed. 'I'm amazed, to be honest. I know Anya gave it a shout-out on her Instagram page, but that doesn't explain all the older people here.'

'I too gave it a "shout-out", but I used the slightly more traditional method of calling people,' Pedro replied. 'I thought you could use some gravitas!' She laughed and hugged him, amazed at how people had pulled together for this cause.

An hour later, when the band had their generator and equipment set up and were doing a quick sound-check, the place was positively heaving. There was a party feel to the atmosphere, and Abi noticed a catering truck had turned up and was doing a roaring trade. The smell of fried onions permeated the air. Pedro's cousin Alexandro was there as promised to report for El Diario Vasco, and he rushed up to her excitedly.

'Abi, Abi,' he called, 'I have good news. I spoke to my contact at CNN en Español, sent her a few pictures of what's going on here, and they are going to send a film crew down!'

'That'll show them. They can't ignore us now, Abi,' May crowed happily as the first guitar chords rang out over the speakers. There was a surge in the crowd as the fans pushed forward. Abi looked on as people started to dance near the front, and she could see even the older generation were tapping their toes along to the poppy beat.

She smiled, wishing fervently that Gabe was here to enjoy this. Abi checked her phone for the hundredth time, but there was still no news from him, so she put it away and tried to put him out of her mind. She couldn't get distracted by this man she barely knew. She had to focus on the here and now and this marvellous event that was erupting around her.

The news crew arrived in a large white van; the channel's loup;go splashed in large red letters along its side. They set up, the camera panning the crowds as the band finished up their set, taking in the undulating crowd. There was a roar of appreciation and the band took a bow, the lead singer blowing kisses out to the crowd as she brought the microphone back to her lips.

'Thank you, thank you,' she bowed graciously. 'Thank you all for coming today to support us in our fight against the property developers and the local council who think it's OK to steamroller this beautiful land behind us.' There were hoots and catcalls from the crowd. 'And we would particularly like to thank Abi. Where are you, girl?' she called out. May pushed Abi forward, and she lurched unwillingly through the crowd.

'Come on up here, so we can thank you properly.'

Abi made her way over, blushing to her roots, as a loud cheer went up, followed by the crashing sound of the crowd clapping. The CNN camera honed in on her, the reporter pushing forward, microphone held out.

'So, we are here with Abigail Johnson, a relative newcomer to our shores who has organised this protest. What made you do this?'

'I...' Abi stumbled over the first words before finding her voice. 'I have always despised these large corporate property developers that think they can just throw money around and do whatever they want,' she said, her eyes shining passionately. 'The fact that they wanted to take this area away from the animals that inhabit it and the kids in that orphanage over there who play on it. Well, I just couldn't stand by and let that happen.'

The reporter was nodding at her but was holding her earpiece, listening to another voice somewhere else. Her face fell slightly before she recovered her composure and asked, 'what would you say if I told you it was too late? We have it on good authority that the sale of the land went through yesterday.'

Abi's heart plummeted, all the positive energy around her dissipating in an instant with this news. The crowd had fallen silent, staring at her accusingly, it seemed. She was speechless in the face of the camera, the reporter poised, waiting for an answer she did not have. Aunt May strode forward, putting a protective arm around her.

'We say that the fight is not over,' May boomed defiantly. 'Let's see them get their machinery in here through us!' she punched the air, and the crowd cheered. Abi looked on in a state of detachment as the reporter finished her piece and the crew bundled back into their van. People kept talking to her, saying positive things like, 'it's not over yet' and 'we'll fight them to the end', but she felt too drained to react. Her exhaustion from the rollercoaster of the last few weeks, coupled with a night of no sleep, finally catching up with her.

May, who was still holding her, said gently, 'come on, Abi. Let's go and have something to eat.' She looked at her niece for a moment. 'No, scrap that. What we need is a drink!'

The drive back into town passed quickly, Abi staring trance-like out of the window and Aunt May gibbering away in an attempt to get through to her. When they walked into the bar, Miquel rushed over and gave her a hug.

'I am sorry, Abi. I saw on the news what happened. And after all your hard work,' he said consolingly.

They sat at a table in silence until Miquel brought their drinks over. 'Let's have a toast,' May held up her glass, her face resolute.

'A toast to what?' Abi asked dismissively. This seemed more like a wake situation than a celebration.

'A toast to the amazing event you pulled together, Abi. Whatever the outcome, you did a fantastic job. Look how many people turned up today! Oh look, there's Pedro.' Her eyes lit up as she watched him walk in, go up to the bar and have an urgent conversation with Miquel. 'I wonder what's up?'

Abi, who had followed her aunt's gaze, saw Miquel look up sharply. He was looking at her with a strange expression, a hint of triumph mixed with something else. He came over to the table and looked down at her.

'I'm sorry to bring you more bad news, Abi. But it seems like the property developer that has bought the land is none other than Gabe Xavier.'

'That's not possible,' she insisted. But her mind was already pulling all the pieces of the puzzle together, running over all the niggling things she knew about him, and her heart was sinking. She pulled her phone out to Google him, and there he was. Successful, smiling, with a string of leggy blondes on his arm. The CEO of Xavier Industries, one of the top-ranking property developers in the States. Tears blurred her vision, and she heard the distant sound of Aunt May saying, 'Oh, Abi. I'm so sorry.'

Blood pounded in her ears as she stood up. 'That bastard!' she said fiercely, her face flushed and her eyes blazing. 'I'm going to give him a piece of my mind.'

She pushed her way out of the bar, ignoring the call from her aunt, and ran down the street, propelled by her anger and mortification. How could she have fallen so easily for his charms? It was obviously just a ploy, a means to an end in his grand scheme. She flew past the carousel and, with shaking hands, opened the street door, almost tripping up the stairs. Banging on the apartment door brought no response.

'Gabe,' she shouted, 'let me in, Gabe!' When there was still no answer, she pulled her keys back out to let herself in. Nothing would stop her from saying her piece. The door swung open, revealing a surprised-looking Gabe in the hallway, his face lighting up when he saw her.

'Abi, I wasn't expecting to see you,' he said, leaning in for a kiss. She pushed him away, hand splayed on his chest, her full force behind it, and he stumbled over his bag, which was on the floor behind him.

'So, you were just going to leave?' she hissed. 'Disappear without a word or an apology?' Her eyes flamed and her cheeks were red. Fury emanated off her in waves.

'I was just about to text you,' he waved his phone at her to prove his point. 'Something has come up, something urgent. I have to get back to New York.'

'Oh, I bet you do. Another good deal come up?' she sniped viciously. 'Maybe there're some puppies that you can steal some land from, huh?'

His face crumpled; brows drawn together in confusion. 'Have you been drinking, Abigail?'

'Not enough to remove the bitter taste from my mouth,' she snapped. 'How could you? How could you deprive those kids of that land? Was taking them out some kind of salve for your guilty conscience? Do you even have a conscience?' She stopped, panting, watching the expression change on his face.

'I was going to tell you...' he started.

'Don't bother, there is nothing you can say that would justify what you have done to them. Or to me, for that matter. But I'm a big girl, I'll get over it.'

He stared at her mutely for a moment, his eyes almost black. 'Is that what you think of me? Do you really think I'd...?'

'Save it, Gabe. Save it for someone who cares.' She looked down at his bag. 'Don't you have a flight to catch?'

Gabe nodded solemnly, handed her the keys to the apartment and pushed past her, walking down the stairs without another word.

He was just like her father, letting you think you meant something to him and then disappearing out of your life. She sank to the floor, tears pouring down her face as she buried it in her knees, soaking her jeans. How could he do this? Not just to her, but to those poor kids? Her complicity in the loss of their playground stabbed her like a knife, and she moaned her grief to the empty hallway.

CHAPTER FIFTEEN

Gabe sat on the plane, heading back to New York. The news that Father Thomas had been rushed into the hospital had superseded every other thing in his world. He looked at his phone and could see they still had three more hours until they touched down. Hopefully, he would be there in time.

His mind was still reeling from the conversation he'd had with Abigail. Not that he had been able to get a word in edgeways. How could she possibly think so little of him? He shook his head at the offer of a drink from the hostess and closed his eyes and tried to sleep.

There hadn't been time to order his usual private jet, his need to get moving too urgent, so he had just booked the first connecting flights he could find out of Spain. The hustle and bustle of the charter flights came as something as a shock to him, and the legroom was downright ridiculous. With his knees practically around his ears, he shifted uncomfortably and, along with the pounding on the back of his seat from the child behind, who was obviously practising to be a drummer, sleep was hard to come by.

When they landed at JFK, everything seemed to take too long. The queue for passport control, the interminable wait for his bag to come lazily gyrating around on the belt. He elbowed his way forward to retrieve it. He wasn't used to this kind of travel and his sense of urgency grew with each frustrating moment. Finally, he was out the doors and into the familiar stale air of the city, and he hailed a taxi to take him to the private clinic he'd had the priest moved to.

He strode into the reception and quickly got the room number. The lift up to his floor was impossibly slow, and his pace quickened as he walked down the hall. Hesitating for just a moment, he pushed the door open, dreading what was waiting on the other side. Father Thomas looked up from his reading in surprise and broke into a smile.

'Gabe, my boy. What on earth are you doing here? You're supposed to be in Spain.'

'You think I could languish around sipping sangria while you're on your deathbed?' he replied, studying the man's face intently from the doorway.

'As you can see,' he glanced down at himself, 'I'm alive and kicking. It was just a nasty bout of bronchitis that laid me low. You're not getting rid of me that easily.' The priest chuckled, laying his book to one side. 'So, come in. Come and tell me all about your adventures.'

Gabe walked in, relief flooding over him. The old man looked pretty good, just a little thinner and paler than usual. He sat on the white leatherette chair in the corner, his body sagging as the tension drained from him, and smiled at Father Thomas.

'I must say, it's a relief to see you looking so well,' he admitted slowly. 'I thought... Well, I thought you might not still be with us,' he finished in a voice strangled with emotion.

'Now, now. I'm going to be busting your balls for a few more years yet, Gabe. But we both know eventually the Lord will call me home.'

'Please don't talk like that,' he replied in a small voice. Father Thomas laughed, a loud, robust sound that echoed around the sterile room.

'Ah, Gabe. It's going to happen one day or another. We can't spend our time worrying about it. That's why I'm always on at you about finding someone to share your life with. I wanna know that there will be someone else to bust your chops when I'm gone.'

Gabe smiled in response, Abigail's face flashing through his mind. Her laugh, the way her lips responded when he kissed her and the way he felt able to tell her anything. He shook these images away, but not before Father Thomas had seen the emotion cross his face. The priest pushed himself up, reaching for a glass of water on the side table, and cocked his head at him.

'What? What was that I just saw? Did you meet someone?'

Gabe stared at him for a long minute before replying.
'I thought I had, if I'm honest. I met a girl in Spain who...' he paused, 'well let's just say she was different. And there was a moment when I thought there might be something there. But, turns out she's just like everyone else and doesn't believe in me and is ready to think the worst.'

'You were only there a few days; how could you possibly have mucked it up so quickly?'

With a sigh, Gabe looked out the window, trying to get his mind in order. It had all happened so suddenly. But he explained it as best he could, and Father Thomas listened carefully without interrupting.

'Well, it sounds to me like she reacted perfectly reasonably,' he said when Gabe had finished his sad tale. Gabe looked at him, hurt.

'Reasonably? She believed I was capable of depriving those poor kids of the land and using her in the process!'

'Of course she did,' he took another sip of water. 'How else would it have looked? Why on earth didn't you tell her from the outset what your plan was?'

Gabe gave it some consideration. There wasn't a valid reason he could think of as to why he hadn't included her in his plans. Just the fact that he was used to working alone, trusting no one. It was a cutthroat business, after all.

'Seems to me, Gabe, that you wouldn't want a woman who wasn't horrified by your apparent actions. Seems to me that she busted your chops, just the way I would have if I had heard such a thing.' The priest smiled at him; his eyes gleaming. 'It also seems to me that the Gabe I know doesn't give up so easily when he wants something,' he finished triumphantly.

Gabe stood and began pacing the room, his mind tumbling through possible scenarios. Should he contact her, try to explain? The thought of not seeing her again was dreadful, but the thought of her rejecting him again was even more terrifying.

'Where's your backbone, man?' the priest barked as if he could read his mind. 'Send the woman a message. You just need the opportunity to talk. That's how we mere mortals deal with these situations.'

Abi had slept fitfully that night and was up before the sun. Even Bob had done no more than ruffle his feathers slightly when she had made her coffee. She sat on the balcony, warming her hands on her cup, and gazed out blankly, trying to sort through her feelings. It was a mixed bag of emotions. Heartbreak being prominent, guilt at what had happened with the land a close second. There was also the worry about her job, the fact that her first guest had left early could reflect badly on her skills as a concierge. She couldn't assume that Gabe would say anything in her defence. Not now. He was obviously capable of anything his cold-hearted soul desired.

She let out a slow breath between pursed lips as she galvanised herself to face the day. There was nothing she could do about him, but she could make sure the guests arriving on Saturday had everything that they had asked for and more. She checked back through the emails on her phone and made a list of everything they had requested in a bid to busy her mind. But memories of their time together, those kisses, kept pushing through and she put her pen down with a sigh.

'I'd ask for a penny for your thoughts,' said May, coming out and taking a seat. 'But I can guess. Mr Unusual?'

'Yes,' Abi sighed exasperatedly. 'I can't believe I got him so wrong,' she said sadly. 'Yet another fine example of a man letting me down, just like dad.'

'It seems to be the case. I'm sorry, love, I had high hopes for you two. But I thought you were going to give your dad a chance? You know, after the conversation we had the other day?'

'I was. I did. I sent him an email, but he hasn't bothered to respond, so I guess he's not that concerned anymore.'

'I'm sure that's not true,' May said firmly. 'Your dad

loves you very much, Abi. Mark my words, he will be in touch as soon as he can. But the best thing to do now is to keep busy. I have to go to the gallery today, to pick up the paintings that are left now the show has finished. Why don't you come with me?'

'That's a good idea. Saves me sitting around moping. Which ones didn't sell?'

'It was the smaller ones, the carousel scenes,' May replied, a frown creasing her brow.

'That's a surprise, they were my favourites,' said Abi. Flashbacks of riding the carousel coursing through her mind, the joy and thrill of letting everything go. 'Listen, I have some calls to make to organise the tours and things that the next guests want, but after that I'm free?'

'Perfect,' her aunt replied. 'I'm just going to pop out and meet Pedro for a quick coffee, then I'll be back.' She stood and gave Abi a kiss on the cheek. 'Don't worry, my love, there's someone out there for you. Someone just as marvellous as you.'

'I'm not so sure about that, May. But thank you.'

Abi made her calls and organised the necessary trips, then emailed the family who would arrive on Saturday to let them know that everything was set up for them. She had just walked into the kitchen when a message popped up on her phone. She stared at it in disbelief. It was from Gabe. She hesitated a moment before clicking on it. What could he possibly have to say at this point?

Can we talk, please?

She shook her head. The audacity of that man. What the hell was left to talk about? Throwing her phone onto the counter, she studiously ignored it as she made a coffee, before walking back out to the balcony. She was still sitting there contemplating her life when she heard May come back in and got up to greet her. She found her in the kitchen, putting away some shopping.

'Hi, May. How is Pedro?'

'He's still wonderful,' her aunt beamed back at her, her face falling when she saw Abi's expression. 'I'm sorry, love.'

'Sorry for what?' she asked with a frown.

'For being so happy, so in love,' she replied, trying to look sombre and failing comically.

'Don't be silly, Aunt May. I'm thrilled for you, I truly am.' She walked over and took her aunt's hands in hers. 'It couldn't have happened to two nicer people.'

'It's just a shame that after you played cupid so well for us and then this happens. I can't believe Mr Unusual just waltzed off like that without a word.' Seeing her angry glance at her phone, May asked, 'what? Has he been in touch?'

'He has messaged,' she admitted. 'He wants to talk. But there's nothing left to say as far as I'm concerned,' she said adamantly, pulling her hands away.

May grabbed her hands back. 'Don't you think it's worth giving him a chance to explain?'

'What possible explanation can there be for his behaviour?'

'Well, remember, you thought the same about your father. When you only know one side of the story, it's easy to make snap judgements,' she said sagely.

Abi glanced at the phone again, doubt clouding her face. Then she shook her head.

'No, May. It is what it is. I don't want to open myself up to more hurt. I'm beginning to think I am better off without a man.'

'Don't say that, love. I know you've been hurt a few times, but we all have. That's part of the risk you take loving someone. And yes, it's horrible, but the upside is so wonderful, it is so wonderfully worth it.'

Seeing her niece wasn't convinced, she let it go and changed tack. 'How about we go and pick up those paintings and then go for lunch?'

'Ok, May, just give me a second to get ready.'

When they arrived at the gallery, the manager bustled up, treating May like royalty after the success of the show. They were soon settled in her office, sipping prosecco, as she gushed about the amazing press and feedback that had surrounded the event.

'Thank you,' May said, looking delighted. 'But you know, it couldn't have happened without Abi here? She did all the promotion; it is thanks to her it was such a success.'

The woman looked at Abi, assessing her intently. 'Well, if you ever want a job, please do let me know,' she smiled. Abi laughed, shaking her head depreciatingly, heat rising to her cheeks.

'I'll bear that in mind. Anyway, we came to pick up the paintings?' she said, moving the conversation on.

The woman's face fell, and she looked back at May. 'Oh, I am so sorry. I should have called you, but it's been so frantic this morning. Someone called and bought them, we shipped them out this morning.'

'Wow, Ok. That's a shame,' she said, turning to Abi. 'I was going to give them to you as a present as you liked them so much.'

'Oh, May. That was a lovely idea, but I'm sure they have gone to a suitable home,' she replied, thinking that the last thing she needed was a constant reminder of Gabe. That first meeting here at the gallery, that had sent fireworks shooting through her body. The night he had pulled her onto the carousel and she had finally let go of her fears and opened up to him. No, she definitely didn't need that hanging on her wall. A constant reminder that she was better off alone and should never open up to anybody.

They went for lunch after the gallery, a new pintxo bar down on the seafront that had been getting rave reviews. But as delicious as the meal looked, her heart just wasn't in it. She listlessly played with the food on her plate, staring out to sea, only vaguely aware of her aunt's chatter. Finally, she said, 'May, do you mind if I go for a walk? I need to get my head straight and try to focus on what I need to do to get through this next couple of days.'

Her aunt smiled at her. 'Of course, sweetheart. No problem, you just go and I'll finish up here. I'll see you back at home?'

Abi nodded and got her bag before kissing her aunt and walking across the road to the beach. May looked on sadly. The poor girl looked so miserable. It was unbearable, but she knew there was nothing she could do to help Abi. Just be there for her when she needed to talk.

Abi walked along the sand, lost in thought. The children happily splashing at the edge of the water, contrasting bleakly with her mood and she tried to recall the last time she'd been happy. *Right here, on this beach, with him*, her inner voice supplied viciously.

'Well, that's not happening again, is it?' she whispered to the world. She could feel her phone in her pocket, the unanswered message nagging at her constantly. Unfinished business. She took it out, opened the message and stared at it, resisting the urge to throw it into the sea. Taking a deep breath, she typed her answer, three little words to convey all these emotions. She hit send and carried on walking joylessly along the water's edge.

Gabe was sitting in his apartment, staring at the screen saver on his computer screen. A montage of moments with Abigail, playing like a cheesy romance movie, on a continuous loop through his mind. Really, he should be in the office right now, getting on top of the work that was piling up, but he didn't have the heart for it. He checked his phone yet again, but she still hadn't responded. He considered sending another message, explaining everything, but shied away from that idea. If she still didn't answer, knowing everything, how would he feel? Heartbroken was the resounding answer, and Gabe Xavier did not do heartbreak. Not anymore.

Snapping back to attention, he tapped the screen back to life. There was an idea he had for moving forward with his business. He was in the position now where he could do what the hell he liked with his money and he was determined to follow this passion inspired by his recent work in San Sebastian. He would still have to work Xavier Industries hard in order to continue to fund his new projects, but he felt the old spark of excitement, the thrill of the chase, returning.

When his phone chimed a while later, he picked it

up distractedly, his mind on the plot of land he had found in Italy. He clicked it open and ice frosted his body as he stared at the three words.

Go to hell.

He sat back, well that was that then. Another woman letting him down when he least deserved it. To hell with her, he told himself as he stood and strode through to the kitchen, pulling a beer out of the fridge and popping off the lid angrily. He leaned against the work surface and took a long gulp, trying to locate the Gabe Xavier attitude of before San Sebastian.

The Gabe that didn't care and did not want to get involved with anyone, but he was struggling to find him. Pushing off the counter, he walked back into the lounge and sat at the computer, determined to lose himself in work. That would rid his mind of thoughts of Abigail Johnson and the hope she had inspired.

CHAPTER SIXTEEN

Friday morning found May and Abi in their usual position on the balcony, drinking coffee and enjoying the warmth of the morning sun. They could hear Bob screeching happily in the distance and Abi hoped the bird wasn't getting up to mischief.

'What's on your schedule today, sweetheart?' May asked, looking with concern at her niece's face. Her pale, blotchy skin and red, heavily bagged eyes told her everything she needed to know about Abi's night. The poor child looked worse than when she had arrived in Spain last month, if that was possible.

'Oh, I think I'll go and do my checks on the apartment, ready for tomorrow's arrival,' she replied without enthusiasm. 'You know, as it's empty…'

May nodded, 'makes sense.'

'That's the one plus,' she snorted without mirth. 'They wanted an early check-in and now they can have it.'

'Every cloud has a silver pining,' May said as gaily as she could. 'I'm going to the protest after lunch. I think you should come too.'

'I'm not sure I'll be welcome there,' said Abi sadly, thinking they must all hate her now after her failed attempt at stopping the sale.

'Don't be ridiculous, girl,' May said sternly. 'What happened with the land is absolutely not your fault. Nobody can hold you to blame. You did an amazing job there.'

'Fat good that did!'

'Abi, pull yourself together and come with me this afternoon. We still need your help if we are going to stop whatever development... *they* are planning.'

'You mean *he's* planning. It's ok, you can say it.' She looked out at nothing for a moment, then said with a sigh, 'but you're right, of course. I should go. I want to go and see Jakinda and apologise for this mess and there's no point in putting that off.'

At El Carrusel, she wandered around listlessly, checklist in hand. The rooms seemed so empty without Gabe in them. He had a way of filling the space, not just because of his physical size. His entire personality filled a room in a way that couldn't be ignored, and now the apartment seemed barren. Her future seemed barren without him in it too, she realised sadly. It didn't take long for her to see that the maid had made everything ship-shape and tomorrow's guests would have nothing to complain about.

She locked up and trudged back up the street, planning to drop off at the small supermarket and give them the pre-arrival shopping list her next guests had sent through. She bumped into Miquel as he came out of the store. 'Abi, hey. How are you?' he asked, brightening as he realised who it was, and then his face falling as he took in her countenance.

She sighed but put a smile on for him. 'I've been better, Miquel. But I'll be ok,' she said bravely. He took her in his arms and gave her a reassuring hug.

'Of course you will,' he said. 'Why don't you come to the bar later and we can talk?'

'Sure,' she replied, pulling away. 'May and I are going to the protest in a bit, but we'll call by afterwards.' She gave him a quick smile and pushed through the door and into the shop. *God, everything is such a struggle,* she thought as she tried to reply to the smiling woman behind the counter, the overriding sense of sadness she felt threatening to erupt in tears at any given moment. Exhausted by the grief she felt, she went back to the apartment. Maybe she would tell May she couldn't go. All she wanted to do was curl up in bed and cry.

'Absolutely not!' was her aunt's response. 'You are coming with me whether you like it or not, Abigail Johnson. Now pull on your big girl pants and let's go and do something useful.'

The atmosphere at the protest was a subdued affair, so different from two days ago. The festival feel had fled and only a handful of serious-looking protesters remained. But they all cheered when the van pulled up, and they gathered around Abi when she arrived, hugging her in welcome, which made her feel a little better. Then she realised they were all staring at her, waiting to see what cunning plan of action she had come up with.

'So, what do we do now?' one of them asked. 'Are we going to have another big rally like before?'

'I… I'm not sure' Abi replied, mind racing guiltily. She hadn't given a thought to their next steps since she'd been so preoccupied with her own woes. She looked over at the orphanage. 'The first thing I am going to do is go and see Jakinda,' she said firmly. 'After that, we can start planning our defence of the area!' There was a small cheer that bolstered her and she walked dejectedly over to the front door and rang the bell. It was answered by Paula, who smiled in greeting and kissed her on both cheeks.

'Welcome, Abi,' the older woman said happily. 'We were hoping you would stop by. Come, Jakinda is in the office.' She led her down a long, dark hallway, the sickly green paint on the walls showing evidence of damp and age, and Abi's heart sunk even further. Maybe I could do some fundraising for the place, she realised with a start. Something good could come out of this horrible situation. A glimmer of hope flared. Perhaps she could do some good here and make up for introducing Gabe into their lives. Jakinda was sitting behind her desk, but jumped up when she saw Abi.

'Good afternoon, Abi. I was just about to call you.'

Abi held up a hand. 'Before you say anything, I just want to apologise,' she said earnestly.

'Whatever for?' the woman asked, looking perplexed.

'Well, for all this nonsense,' she replied expansively, waving a vague arm. 'You know, for Gabe Xavier. Losing the land. Honestly, I had no idea what he was up to.' She hurried on, talking over Jakinda's response. 'I would never have brought him here if I had known what a bastard he was.' She finished fiercely, tears sliding down her face.

A small smile played over the woman's face. 'Ah, I see. Please, take a seat,' she said, pulling a chair in front of her desk then returning to her own. 'Paula, could you give us a moment?'

As the door closed behind the departing woman, Jakinda pulled open a draw and snapped a tissue from inside, handing it to her silently. Abi dabbed at her face and tried to get her emotions in check. These people had far greater things to worry about than a broken heart.

When she could see that the girl had regained some composure, Jakinda started softly, 'Abi, you have nothing to apologise for.'

Abi's head shot up; eyes bright. 'Of course I do. I

should have known he was a property developer. Hell, if I had been doing my job properly, I would have researched him harder before he came, but I didn't. I'm useless,' she finished lamely, shrinking back into her seat, tears welling again.

Jakinda stood and walked over to the window, staring thoughtfully out at the protesters in the distance and the land beyond. Seeming to reach a decision, she turned, looking down at her seriously.

'Can I trust you with something, Abi?' she asked.

Taken aback, Abi replied uncertainly, 'Ah, yes. I mean, yes, of course.'

'Gabe Xavier did indeed buy the land two days ago. But yesterday his lawyers contacted me and he has gifted the land to the orphanage. I'm going into town tomorrow to sign the paperwork.'

Abi stared at her, her mouth hanging open, mind racing, unable to respond for a moment.

'But... But...' Abi was speechless. She had been so convinced he was an evil, cold-hearted property developer with nothing in mind other than making money. This new version of him was impossible to comprehend.

'Why the hell didn't he say something?' she finally asked.

'I gather he wanted to keep it quiet. If his competitors had got wind of his interest in the land, they would automatically have thrown their hats in the

SUMMER IN SAN SEBASTIAN

ring, driving up the price. He is a businessman after all,' she chuckled, taking her seat again. 'So, you see, Abi. You have nothing to feel bad about. You bringing him here was a boon in more ways than one.'

'There's more?' Abi asked, her face still twisted in confusion.

'Yes, his original intent was just to get the land for us. But when he saw the bedraggled state of the home, he also donated what you can only call a pretty hefty sum to us. We can now renovate this building, and he is also flying over an architect and a building team to help us get it done. He doesn't want any publicity, though; he was adamant about that.'

Abi was flabbergasted and was struggling to take it all in. She stood and paced the room as different thoughts swirled around her brain. Gabe was a cold-hearted bastard. Now he was good? How could this be? Round and round it went in ever-decreasing circles until she reached the inevitable conclusion. He had still gone running off when the deal was done. Something more important had come up. And it hadn't been her. She slumped back in her seat.

'Why don't you look happy? I thought this news would thrill you?' Jakinda asked, looking perplexed.

'Oh, I am,' Abi looked up at her, a smile breaking out. 'I am thrilled for you and the kids. It's just, well... It's just that I had reason to believe we had something going. But he rushed off so suddenly. I presumed it was because he had finished his dastardly deed here and was on to the next thing. But if he was doing all this good, as you say, there was no reason for him to run away.' *Away from you*, her inner voice pointed out needlessly.

'I believe he had to go back to New York because a friend was taken ill? His assistant emailed me yesterday and said he would be out of the office for a few days because of that.'

The rest of the conversation was a blur to Abi. Hopefully, her responses had made sense. But her mind had been replaying that last conversation with him in the doorway. The conversation where she hadn't given him a chance to speak. The conversation where she had angrily assumed he was letting her down, just like every other man in her life, and deserved no more of her time.

May looked over as she saw Abi walking slowly back and could see immediately that something had changed. 'What? What's up? Did they give you a hard time in there?' she asked, rushing over, ready as always to defend her.

'No,' Abi grimaced. 'No, they didn't. Surprisingly, they only had good things to say.' She turned to the group of protesters and called out, 'can I have your attention, please?' A murmur of translation ran through the crowd, and they all looked at her expectantly.

'I am happy to announce that there is no longer any need for our protest,' she said with a smile. 'It seems that the developer who bought this land is not planning to do anything with it. There will be no building work going on here.' There was a slight delay as they translated the message, like Chinese whispers, then a loud cheer went up.

'How can we be sure?' a querulous voice called out from the back, to a murmur of agreement.

'Don't worry. They've, um… they've signed something to that effect, so you can all go home.' The crowd milled about, huddled in small groups, muttering to one another.

'They don't know what to do with themselves now,' May laughed, then leaning in, whispered, 'what the hell is going on?'

'I'll tell you on the way back,' Abi hissed. By the time they had reached their usual parking space in town, Abi had brought May up to speed on what had happened and, of course, sworn her to secrecy.

'I don't understand all this need for cloak and dagger,' she said as they walked towards the bar. 'You would think he would want the world to know about his good deeds.'

'I don't know what his reasoning is,' Abi replied, holding the door open for May. 'I guess we'll never know,' she said sadly. May looked at her sharply.

'What do you mean, child? Now we know he's not the big, mean, baddie we thought he was, there's no reason for you not to follow this up.'

'Do you think I should?' she asked as they sat at a

table, waving to Miquel behind the bar.

'Of course!' May erupted. 'You, my girl, have never shone so brightly as after that night you spent with him on the beach. You were positively glowing with happiness. That, surely, has to be worth fighting for?'

'Do you think it's a good idea?' Abi asked, hope sparking in her eyes. 'Is there any point? I mean, we have very different lives and let's face it, the men in my life to date have needed very little excuse to give up on me. Let alone thousands of miles.'

Abi's mind was racing. Could she let go of her fears of abandonment and give Gabe another chance? Her heart quailed at the idea of going through that kind of pain again. Memories flooded back of her dad, calmly announcing one morning that he was going to live somewhere else, his suitcases already packed and waiting by the front door. The shock at that seemingly sudden statement had knocked her sideways, and she had never recovered from its impact.

Then she thought about Gabe, the way he had felt in her arms and how free she had felt riding the carousel with him, and she knew in her heart that she needed to see him again.

'I should go to New York,' she announced, surprising herself. Then her face fell. 'But, of course, I can't. I have a job to do here, I have guests arriving tomorrow.'

'Don't be daft, I can meet your guests for you.'

Abi looked at her aunt thoughtfully, musing on the

options. 'How's it going to look to Sublime Retreats, though? My first guest leaving early, then me gaily running off to the States when my second guests are due.' She shook her head. 'I can't risk losing my job, can I?'

'I think love is worth a little risk, don't you?' May asked her with a smile.

CHAPTER
SEVENTEEN

The rattling of the little blue carry-on bag May had lent Abi echoed loudly in the early morning air as they walked down the street to where the campervan was parked. Doubts plagued her mind. Was she actually about to throw everything to the wind and go chasing after a man she barely knew? She wasn't sure what her biggest fear was; the thought of losing another job or the idea that he might not want her now. She stopped in her tracks.

'What the hell am I doing? This is crazy!'

'Yes, it is,' her aunt replied, looking at her sternly. 'Let's just turn around and go home to bed'

'What?'

'I said, let's give up this folly and go home, where you can look forward to growing old gracefully. Alone.'

'But... But I don't want to,' Abi whispered.

'Well, there's your answer right there, young lady. Now, come along, you have a plane to catch.'

They loaded themselves into the van and strapped themselves in. May looked across at her.

'Ready?'

Abi nodded. 'Yes, I am,' she replied as May turned the key. The van spluttered and then died. She tried again with the same result. 'Oh, darnation,' her aunt said crossly, 'not now, Bessie.' She took off her seatbelt and pulled a lever under the dash before climbing out and walking to the back of the van to look helplessly at the engine.

'What are we looking for?' asked Abi, who had joined her.

'I have absolutely no idea,' May laughed. 'I was hoping something would, you know, leap out at me. A loose wire or something?'

Abi checked her phone for the time. It was getting late, and she looked around to see if there were any taxis.

'Is there something I can help you ladies with?' came a deep voice from behind them. A voice she remembered so well. Abi spun around in shock.

'Dad?' she cried out. 'Oh my God, what are you doing here?'

'I decided after reading your email that writing

back just wouldn't be enough. I hopped on the first plane I could, so here I am, Sunshine.'

He opened his arms, and she ran to them, years of missing him erupting in tears that ran freely down her face. He held her tightly for several minutes before May interrupted.

'As touching as this is, don't you have a plane to catch?'

She pulled away slightly and looked up at him in concern. 'She's right, Dad. I was just leaving to go to the airport.' She looked over at May, her face haunted with indecision. 'Maybe this is another sign I shouldn't go. What with Bessie giving up the ghost and dad arriving on top of everything else... '

'Don't be ridiculous. Rob, turning up just in the nick of time, proves that you are on the right path. You'll drive her to the airport, won't you?' she arched an enquiring brow at the man who had once been the love of her sister's life. He laughed in response.

'As crazy as ever, May? There's always an adventure going on with you. What have you got my daughter caught up in?'

'Oh, Abi is quite capable of getting caught up in adventures all by herself, don't you worry,' said May almost proudly. 'But this particular one concerns the possibility of love.'

Rob looked at his daughter's face, and the consternation etched there. 'In that case, what are we waiting for?' he asked, pulling a set of keys out of his pocket. 'My hire car is just over there. Grab your bag and you can tell me all about it on the way.'

It felt so strange being in a car again with her father. She couldn't remember the last time. Well, if she was honest, she could. It had been at the funeral, but Abi didn't want to dwell on that now.

'I can't believe you're here,' she said, glancing across at him in amazement, noticing the deep lines that now marked his face. Rob broke into a broad smile.

'Me neither,' he chuckled, his eyes flicking across to her before returning to the road ahead. 'I have been waiting so long for you to reach out to me, Abi. I didn't know if I would ever see you again.'

Tears pricked her eyes as she thought of all the time they had lost. And all because she had overreacted in her usual, stubborn way. Not giving him a chance to explain and tell his side of the story. Exactly like she had with Gabe. No wonder he had walked off without another word.

The journey was over far too swiftly for Abi, who wanted nothing more than to spend time with her dad. But she knew she had to go and find Gabe first and try to explain herself. Hopefully, he would give her another chance.

'I'm sorry, Dad,' she said as they pulled up outside of the departure terminal.

'What for?' Rob asked, smiling at her.

She blew a strand of hair out of her eyes with a long breath. 'For everything. For not listening to you all those years ago, not giving you a chance. And for this.' She waved at the airport building. 'Running off after you went to all the trouble of coming here to see me. I feel terrible.'

He undid his seatbelt and leaned over to give her a hug. She leant into his embrace, the familiar scent of him nearly making her cry again.

'Don't you worry,' he said into her hair. 'We'll have plenty of time when you get back in a couple of days. I'll still be here. If May doesn't drive me mad, that is.'

Laughing, she pulled away, wiping her eyes with her sleeve. 'Thanks, Dad. I'm looking forward to it,' she said with a sniff. She looked at the stream of people walking into the airport, tugging their luggage behind them. 'Well, this is it, I guess,' she said uncertainly, not moving.

'You get out there, girl,' Rob said. 'From what you've told me, it's the right thing to do.'

Nodding, she opened the door and stepped out onto the pavement, waiting while he got her bag from the boot. He handed it to her and gave her another quick squeeze.

'See you soon, Sunshine.'

Abi walked towards the door and, with one last smile back at him, joined the throng of travellers heading into the building. After a three-hour layover in Madrid, she was finally on her way to New York. Abi couldn't believe she was doing this. Leaving her job and her father behind on a fool's errand to follow her heart. She only hoped she could find Gabe when she got there. She had the address for his office, but that was it. Beyond that, she didn't know what else to do. She had tried calling him once, but his phone was off, and in truth, she wanted to see his face. See his reaction when he saw her. Then she would know for sure how he felt.

'What the hell are you doing here?' Gabe demanded as he barged into the office at the orphanage. Father Thomas looked up, unperturbed by the outburst.

'And good morning to you too, Gabe,' he said mildly, with a smile from his seat behind the old wooden desk.

'You are supposed to be taking things easy,' he continued indignantly in the face of the old man's irritating mildness.

'I am. I am taking things easy,' he replied, waving a piece of paper at him. 'See? Just a little paperwork, no need to get overexcited.'

Gabe slumped into the chair in front of the desk, looking around the familiar, tired-looking room in exasperation. How many times had he sat in here as a kid? In trouble for causing mischief, or hearing the familiar "it's not you, it's them" speech when he was dumped unceremoniously back at the orphanage. Memories washed over him and he tried to shake them away, refusing to let them take over.

'I think a better question is, what are *you* doing here? I thought you would be flying back to Spain to sort things out with that girl of yours.'

Gabe blanched at the idea, his face becoming drawn as he recalled the last text from Abigail.

'I think it's safe to say that horse has bolted, Father.'

'Gabe Xavier giving up? Now, there's a thing,' the priest replied with a chuckle of amusement, an impish gleam in his eyes. 'I shall have to make a note of that somewhere, for surely it's a first?'

Ignoring the sarcasm, Gabe said, 'sometimes you have to know when to quit. I learnt that early on in business. There's no point in investing too much into something if you don't think it will bring the returns.'

Father Thomas looked at him sharply. 'You're not honestly comparing love to a business deal, are you?' he asked, surprise crossing on his face.

'For sure, it's the same. You assess the possibilities of getting what you want and make your moves accordingly,' Gabe responded glibly. 'If you think the deal isn't going to pan out, you withdraw, hold your head up high and move on to the next one. It's how I have survived so far!'

Tutting and shaking his head in disapproval, Father

Thomas stood and came around, perching on the edge of the desk in front of Gabe and looking earnestly down at him.

'Love is more like, oh, I don't know, catching a butterfly, let's say. You see something beautiful just ahead, the possibility of owning such a thing spurs you on. You can't just stomp over there with your net and expect the butterfly to just rush straight into it. If it's got any sense, it will just fly away.' He paused for breath, mulling over his next words. 'But if you sincerely want the magical thing, you have to be there. You have to put yourself out there. Even though there is a strong possibility you won't catch it, you never know until you try.'

Laughing despite himself, Gabe said, 'I'm not sure how that works as an analogy, Father, but I get the gist.' He stood and gave him a long hug, the frailness of the old man's frame startling and reminding him why he had come.

'You need to go home,' he said doggedly. 'Rest, eat, and relax. Give your body time to recover.'

'For sure, I will in a bit,' he said, standing to return to his seat. 'I have just a little more to do and then I promise to go home, but only if you think about what I have said?'

'Make sure you do. And I will. I'm flying out to Italy tonight to look at some more land, but I will take some time to think things through before I go,' he promised with a small smile. 'Although I'm not sure there's any point.'

'Courage is like love: it must have hope for nourishment,' the old man recited.

'Bible quote?' Gabe asked.

'Nope, Napoleon. An interesting character, you remind me of him a little. A brilliant mind, excellent tactician, but behind that battle-hardened façade is someone who just wants to be loved.'

Gabe grimaced a little at this truth, but nodded in acknowledgement before walking out the door.

Despite his promise to Gabe, Father Thomas was still in his office two hours later when the door was pushed hesitantly open by a young, red-headed girl who looked at him with enormous eyes that could evidently use some sleep.

'Can I help you, Miss?' he asked gently, her distress becoming more obvious as she entered the room, pulling a small suitcase behind her.

'I hope so...' she hesitated, glancing around the room, her eyes alighting on the four small paintings that hung in a slightly uneven row behind the priest.

'I'm looking for Gabe Xavier. I was told at his office he might be here?'

'Ah, his Josephine,' the priest muttered under his breath before replying to her directly. 'I'm afraid you have missed him. He was here earlier, but he left.'

'Oh,' her face fell as she uttered the tiny word, and

she looked altogether lost.

'Come, take a seat,' he said, his heart going out to her, and he stood and gestured to the chair where Gabe had sat just hours before. She hesitated for a moment, then came in fully and sank gratefully into the seat, staring at the bright colours of the carousel scenes.

Father Thomas studied her. Her face was pale and drawn against the vivid red of her hair, but he could see why Gabe was so taken with her. Her natural beauty shone through despite her pallor and her eyes still held a spark of something determined, even in the face of the exhaustion she was experiencing.

'They were meant for you,' Father Thomas said, turning in his seat to follow her gaze. 'But... Well, Gabe felt he had to find a new home for them, and so here they are.' He looked around the rest of the room. 'They highlight the fact I need to decorate this place,' he chuckled.

'Do you have any idea where he might be?' she asked hopefully, eyes bright with unshed tears. He let out a long breath as he considered her question.

'Well, I know he's planning to fly to Italy tonight,' he said thoughtfully, looking at her as she gasped in dismay. 'But I believe he was going somewhere to think about things. You knocked him for six, you know. That poor boy believed he'd finally found someone he could trust to be himself with.'

The tears were now sliding down her face as she

looked down at her hands, twisting her fingers together on her lap. 'I know, I know,' she murmured, then looked directly at him. 'But I thought he'd done the most heinous thing... I didn't stop to listen. I should have let him explain' she sighed exasperatedly. 'I'm not known for carefully thinking things through,' she said, a brief smile appearing across her face.

'Well, Gabe thinks everything through, and that's what he's doing now. I suggest you go and find him before he thinks himself out of the fact that he's in love with you.'

Her mouth formed a small O of surprise at his words, her face wondrous at the possibility.

'Maybe you could start at his apartment?' he asked, scribbling down the address on a scrap of paper and sliding it across the worn surface of the desk. She reached out to take it but was shaking her head even as she stuffed it into her pocket.

'No, if he's thinking, I know where he will be,' she said decisively and stood up with renewed energy.

Outside the orphanage she hailed a taxi, bundling herself and her bag in and rapidly telling the driver where she wanted to go. She only hoped she was right and would find Gabe before he jetted off to Italy. She couldn't bear the notion she might miss him. The traffic was backed up; the journey took forever, and Abi felt like screaming. When they eventually arrived, she threw some notes at the driver and hurled herself out of the cab, running through the entrance, and after a brief glance at the map, heading to where she hoped she would find him.

The subdued lighting and the flickering of the water continually undulating provided a haven for Gabe's frantic mind. He stared at the tiny creatures, effortlessly gliding from one strand of seagrass to the next, thinking how simple life must be for them. Was Father Thomas right? Should he rush back to Spain and confront Abigail? Follow his heart instead of his head for once? The thought terrified him. He had fallen for her so hard, so quickly, it was impossible to imagine what damage she could inflict on him if he pursued this any further. Gabe looked at the time. He ought to get back to his apartment and pack again for the next trip.

'They mate for life, you know?' said a familiar voice behind him, causing him to straighten up. It couldn't be, could it?

She continued, 'and it's said that if one of the pair dies, or runs away in this case, the remaining one goes into decline, sometimes they even die. It's like they're heartbroken.'

She reached out to touch his shoulder, and he turned slowly to look at her. As the lights played across her beautiful face, she smiled up at him.

'It's like they're heartbroken - because they are.'

'I had to leave, Father Thomas...' he trailed off.

'I know. Well, I know that now. You should have told me.'

'You didn't give me much of a chance,' he grinned, remembering her wrath. Even when she was angry and shouting at him, she was still beautiful.

She returned his grin. 'That is one of my flaws. One of my many, many flaws,' she said, stepping a little closer to him. 'Overreacting, not giving people a chance to explain themselves,' she carried on, thinking about her father and how wonderful it had been to talk with him on the way to the airport.

'But I'm working on it. On them. And if you'll have me, I would like to work on them with you.'

Her eyes shone with hope as she gazed up at him, and he felt overwhelmed with emotion as he bent his head to kiss her. When they pulled apart, he said, 'I must be mad taking on a fixer-upper like you.'

She let out a peal of laughter that rang through the quiet hall of the aquarium and made his heart soar.

'Because you're so perfect?' she inquired sweetly, an eyebrow arched and her lip twitching in amusement.

His dimple flashed as he replied, 'Oh yes. Gabe Xavier has no known flaws. But he does, it appears, have one fatal attraction,' and as their lips met again, he drew her in close, vowing to never let her go.

CHAPTER EIGHTEEN

As the small, private jet bumped down on the tarmac, Abi looked across at Gabe with a smile. 'Home at last,' she said happily. The trip to Brindisi in Italy had been amazing. It was such a beautiful country that after he had completed the deal on the property and land that was being sold out from under the orphanage housed there, they had travelled on up to Florence and stayed in the Sublime Retreats apartment while exploring the city.

There was a flash of guilt as she thought about the company. They had let her go, of course, when she hadn't returned to Spain and news filtered back to them. But Anya had stepped into the role of concierge, and by all accounts was doing well. Abi would just have to think about finding some more work now she was back, but she was far too happy right now to worry about it.

But she had missed Aunt May and, more importantly, was looking forward to spending time with her dad, who was still in San Sebastian patiently waiting for her to return.

'After all these years, a few more days isn't going to make a difference,' he had laughed when she had called him to apologise. 'Anyway, it's about time I had a holiday. I haven't had a break for years, and quite honestly, I am having a whale of a time with May. I had forgotten how much fun she is!'

So, she and Gabe had strolled around Florence, hand in hand, discovering the sights and each other. Taking their time to get to know each other in the sunlit cobbled streets, slowly learning to open up over plates of delicious pasta and reveal their true selves with a glass of wine on the rooftop terrace of the apartment. It had been an amazing few days, but she was happy to be back. To be home.

They walked out of the airport into the brilliant summer morning and Abi heard a voice call out, 'there's my Sunshine.' She followed the sound to where her dad and aunt were waiting for them. With a whoop, she abandoned her bag and ran over, throwing herself into his arms. Aunt May, who stood back to allow them this moment, cocked her head at Gabe as he came over with the bags.

'Mr Unusual, I presume?'

Gabe laughed; he knew all about his nickname. 'Mad Aunt May, I presume?' he replied with a cheeky grin.

'Touché. And welcome to the family. Seems like you'll fit right in!'

Gabe felt a surge of emotions and just nodded in response, unable to articulate how he was feeling. The small boy he had once been still trying to keep a lid on these feelings of hope. Had he finally found his family?

Abi and her dad finally let go of each other, and Rob, looking distinctly glassy-eyed, said, 'Well, kids. Shall we get going?'

Abi nodded and turned to see the campervan parked a little further up the road. 'You got Bessie going again?' she asked, looking at May in delight.

'Of course, sweetheart. I wasn't going to give up on her after all this time!'

The ride back to town was filled with excited chatter and laughter as they caught up, Gabe slowly finding his feet with them and joining in the banter. They headed to the bar for lunch to celebrate the reunion and were greeted by Pedro and then Miquel, who pushed through them all to hug Abi.

'Welcome home, Abi,' he grinned, the broad smile on his handsome face disappearing only for a moment when he turned and saw Gabe. He stretched his hand out. 'And welcome back, Gabe. It's good to see you.'

'Thanks, Miquel,' Gabe replied, slightly surprised, but shaking the proffered hand firmly.

'Come,' Miquel said, turning to include them all. 'Sit. I think this calls for some champagne, don't you?'

They looked around the bar that was relatively empty at this time before the lunchtime rush and selected a table in the corner.

'So, Abi,' said May when they were settled. 'What are your plans now you're back?'

'Well, my priority is finding another job,' she flushed and glanced at Pedro. 'I am so sorry for letting you down, Pedro.'

'Think nothing of it, child,' he replied simply. 'Anya is loving the role, so it all worked out.'

'Besides,' said aunt May, looking lovingly at him. 'We have something else we would like you to organise.'

'Oh, are you doing another exhibition?' Abi asked in surprise.

'No,' she laughed, 'not yet, at least. We want you to organise our wedding!' she beamed at the handsome man sitting next to her whose face reflected her joy.

Abi choked up. 'Oh, May, Pedro. That's wonderful news,' she cried, reaching across the table to grasp their hands in hers and squeeze them both tight.

'Perfect timing,' Rob looked up as Miquel arrived at the table with the champagne, and once they all had a glass, he stood.

'I'd like to make a toast,' he said seriously, looking at

each of them in turn. 'To love, family and happiness!'

Six months later, on a crisp winter morning, May and Pedro were married in a small, simple ceremony at San Sebastian's City Hall, a beautiful old building at the edge of the park that housed the carousel. May looked stunning in a soft grey silk dress that ruched gently down to her knees, and her silver flats had a little sparkle on them. Pedro, as handsome as ever, stumbled over his words a little during his vows. His description of never thinking he would experience love again after he was widowed and his joy at meeting May had them all wiping their eyes.

Gabe held Abi's hand throughout the ceremony, giving it an extra squeeze of support when happy tears rolled down her cheeks. She glanced at his handsome face, still in awe of this man who had swept her off her feet and shown her how to love. They were still working on their flaws. For sure, it wasn't all plain sailing, but together they were getting there.

The reception was a grander affair, and being held at the gallery. Abi had approached them to see if it was possible to have the party there and they had not only said yes, but also offered her a job, which she had gladly accepted. She looked around now, smiling at all the familiar faces who had come to celebrate with them. May and Pedro were much loved, and the room was full to bursting with well-wishers.

She searched for Gabe in the throng and saw him with Jakinda from the orphanage. Diego was next to him, holding on to a trouser leg. Since they had been back, Gabe had spent a lot of time with the boy. He seemed to have a strong bond with him, and Diego had bloomed under his attention. No longer the solemn-faced child that they had first met, he now beamed happily around the room with the cheeky grin she had come to know and love. May came over, practically skipping, her face flushed with happiness and champagne.

'Abi, dear. Thank you so much, this is a fantastic party. Look at what a wonderful time everyone is having!'

Abi had to agree. The crowd seemed to be enjoying themselves very much and she could see the band that had helped at the protest were getting ready to go on stage. Miquel was in the corner with Lisette, who never seemed to be very far away from him these days, and she was fairly confident that they were an item now.

'It was my pleasure, May,' she replied, giving her aunt a big hug. 'And I want to thank you, too.'

'Whatever for, child?'

'For all this,' she waved an arm to take in everything. 'For my new life. Gabe, my dad...' she trailed off, unable to express herself. May carefully tucked an errant strand of her niece's hair behind an ear and said, 'Abi, you have no one to thank but yourself. You were the one brave enough to make the leap, to come to this country, to talk to your dad and go chasing halfway around the world to let Gabe know how you felt. I was happy to support you on your journey, but the credit lies entirely at your feet.'

Abi nodded, her face clenched in a smile, trying not to cry again. She'd only just repaired her make-up from the last time.

When she walked home hand in hand with Gabe later that evening, they agreed that it had been a wonderful party and a fitting way to celebrate May and Pedro's marriage. They paused by the carousel in front of the building where Gabe had bought an apartment for them.

'Abi,' he blurted, looking at her seriously, his face a mask of concern. 'There is something I want to tell you.'

Her heart stuttered for a moment. Was this it? Her inbuilt distrust of the happiness she had been feeling these last few months was throwing up all kinds of horrible scenarios in an instant. Was this the point where he announced he was leaving? Her fight-or-flight instinct shouted at her to get in there first, say something before he could tell her what was on his mind. But she paused, restraining herself as best she could, and just looked up at him with a small smile of enquiry, her heart racing uncomfortably.

'I have been talking with Jakinda and I would like to adopt Diego.' He looked so petrified as he said it, and she couldn't help but laugh.

'Oh, Gabe. I think that's an amazing idea. Why on earth do you look so worried?'

'Well, it's a decision that affects the both of us, isn't it?' he still seemed nervous and was fiddling with his jacket pocket.

'Well, yes,' she said slowly, 'I guess it does, but if *you* want to adopt Diego, that's your decision at the end of the day.'

'That's just it,' there was a slight wobble in his voice. 'I don't just want me to adopt him, I want *us* to.'

And with that, he dropped to one knee and pulled a small blue box out of the pocket he had been fiddling with.

'Abigail Johnson, will you do me the ultimate honour of marrying me?' he asked, flipping open the lid to reveal the sparkling diamond ring inside. The rush of joy that coursed through her made Abi throw back her head and laugh out loud before nodding down at his worried face and answering him.

'Yes, Gabe, I would like nothing more than to become Mrs Xavier!'

AFTERWORD

Thank you so much for reading my book. I hope you enjoyed it as much as I enjoyed the time spent bringing it all together! As a savvy shopper you will know the importance of reviews. Please take a moment to share your thoughts with me on any of these platforms...

Amazon, GoodReads, BookBub

WANT TO KEEP IN TOUCH?

YOU CAN SIGN UP FOR MY NEWSLETTER ON MY WEBSITE: JOYSKYE.COM FOR A CHANCE TO WIN A COPY OF ONE OF THE NEW BOOKS, AND UPDATES ON NEW RELEASES.

TO CHECK OUT MY SOCIALS:

FACEBOOK @JOYSKYEAUTHOR **INSTAGRAM** @JOYS.KYE **TWITTER** @JOYSKYE4 **BOOKBUB** JOY SKYE

Printed in Great Britain
by Amazon